Githa Hariharan was educated in Bombay, Manila and the United States where she also worked in public television. Since 1979, she has worked in Bombay, Madras and New Delhi, first as an editor in a publishing house, then as a freelancer. *The Thousand Faces of Night* won the Commonwealth Writers Prize for the best first novel. Githa Hariharan has also published *The Art of Dying*, a collection of her stories; another novel, *The Ghosts of Vasu Master*; and edited *A Southern Harvest*, an anthology of short stories. Her stories have appeared in magazines and journals internationally, and 'The Remains of the Feast' was included in the anthology, *In Other Words: New Writing by Indian Women* (The Women's Press, 1993).

The
Thousand
Faces
of
Night

GITHA HARIHARAN

Published in Great Britain by The Women's Press Ltd, 1996
A member of the Namara Group
34 Great Sutton Street, London EC1V 0DX

First published in India by Penguin Books India, 1992

British Library Cataloguing-in-Publication Data
A catalogue record for this book is available from the British Library

ISBN 0 7043 4465 3

Printed and bound in Great Britain by
BPC Paperbacks Ltd

For my parents

Suppose you cut a tall bamboo
in two;
make the bottom piece a woman,
the headpiece a man;
rub them together
till they kindle:
　　　　　tell me now,
the fire that's born,
Is it male or female,
　　　　　O Ramanatha?
　　　　　—*vachana* by Devara Dasimayya,
translated from the Kannada by A.K. Ramanujan

Prelude

I have always liked the story that comes whole and well-rounded, complete with annotation. But mostly I have come across the sharp, jagged, tip-of-the-iceberg variety, and I have always been foolish enough to ask a question.

I must have asked my grandmother Why? thousands of times. She must have answered me; there were few questions she could resist.

But I was a child then, and the answers I now reconstruct were perhaps never really hers. Perhaps I put the oracular, paradoxical words into her generous, buck-toothed mouth each time I recall the fables of childhood.

What I do remember, with greater certainty, are the words of a more recent, pragmatic storyteller.

When I once asked my husband's housekeeper, old Mayamma, why she had put up with her life, she laughed till the tears rolled down her wrinkled cheeks.

'I can see that you are still a child,' she said.

'When I lost my first baby, conceived after ten years of longing and fear, I screamed, for the only time in my life, Why?

'The oily, pock-marked village doctor, his hand still dripping with my blood, looked shifty. A woman must learn to bear some pain, he mumbled. What can I do about the sins of your previous birth?

'But my mother-in-law was far more sure of herself. She slapped my cheeks hard, first this then the other. Her fists pummelled my breasts and my still swollen stomach till they had to pull her off my cowering, bleeding body. She shouted, in a rage mixed with fear, "Do you need any more proof that this is not a woman? The barren witch has killed my grandson, and she lies there asking us why!" '

Mayamma smiled toothlessly at me, as if the memory had lost some of its bite.

'So be careful, Devi,' she chuckled, her mouth sucking in gulps of air like a fish, 'when you next ask a question.'

PART ONE

1

It was November, with two weeks to go for her journey back to India. To a Madras far from this wintry postcard landscape, sheathed in the muted greys and whites that muffled the discordant notes of decision so effectively.

Soon, thought Devi, I will stand on dry, cracked soil burnt brown by a merciless sun. I will shut my eyes and see a fire that burns a glowing amber, that turns liquid and rolls down my back in cool, refreshing streams of sweat.

Two weeks to pack, to cram her bulging, inadequate suitcases full of mementoes; two weeks to shut them tight in the airless recesses of her memory. She thought very little of what lay ahead. Her time was filled with reassuring rituals, items on her check-list, each to be neatly crossed out once accomplished; each ready then for cold storage, to be drawn out and examined in the warm safety and relentless light of the Indian sun.

Devi's last day in America, promised to Dan, found her in a state of hectic euphoria. Dan was waiting for her at an open air café, the Hasselblad that followed him around like a faithful dog lying on the chair next to him. He took photographs of her wherever they went. Later, in the darkroom, he would gloat over his collection of exotica. Today, he did not greet her by peering into the viewfinder.

The imminent journey seemed to have played a trick on their roles: now she looked at him as if she were the photographer, he the subject.

She looked at his hair, at the millions of tightly wound springs of black wool that never failed to take her by surprise. The first time she had touched his hair, she had momentarily braced her hand for a feeling of coarseness, rough and comforting. She had, instead, strayed out of her depth, her fingers trembling in this furry wood where everything was softness, dark and alluring; so honey-sweet and insidiously seductive.

They had a long, leisurely brunch, and the cold white wine flowed down Devi's throat like some magic stream, all ripples and sparks in a haze of sunshine. Dan was gentle, charming, determined that this should be a day for her to take back in remembrance.

Dan was Devi's answer to the white claustrophobia of an all-clean, all-American campus. Even before they could come together in friendship, approach romance, a link had formed itself between them across the classroom, a bond forged on the fringes of middle-class, vitamin-popping, milk-drinking America.

Since then, the bond had grown. Promises had been half-made in the dark shadows of the parking lot outside the grimy, friendly diner they often met at. But all along, Devi had clearly relegated this relationship to the blurred regions of fantasy. The purple-hued, velvety black of his skin; the dazzling white smile of his sensual teeth; the soft voice sometimes deliberately assuming the repetitious, singsong talk of the ironical black man flaunting his identity: all these were the tantalizing images of some alien mirage, some barely remembered dream of clandestine passion.

The dream was shattered every time she met Dan with his friends. Neither family had come into the picture—his was not important enough as far as he was concerned. Hers was far too important, far too precious, to be subjected to the humiliation of

3

being transplanted in these shores where anything was possible. The last time she had gone with Dan to meet some friends of his in a neighbouring state campus, she had brimmed with anticipation and good intentions. She would shed her inhibitions, her burden of Indianness, and merge with these oases of colour and spontaneity which relieved the monotony of an anaesthetized suburbia.

The room was full of people, young black men and women, even a few children. As her apprehension grew into a sudden shyness, Devi reassured herself that this was just like India—the throng of voices competing with the loud, blaring music, the high-pitched voices of excited children in the background.

They spoke to each other, over the music, in a shorthand that fascinated Devi, but she could not bring herself to play impostor and speak like them.

The more serious conversations, carried out in little huddles in various corners of the room, were about being black in white America. Devi leaned forward to listen to an intense young woman with a spectacular head of a hundred little plaits. Her frizzy, snake-like braids were held in place with blue and green beads at regular intervals.

'So this nurse—all polite and freezing cold—I had paid for the hospital room, see—said, "I'll take the baby to the nursery for the night, you get some rest alone." She didn't want me to be disturbed by my baby. "Disturbed!" I screamed into her icy face. "When are you people going to learn that black love is black wealth?" '

Devi saw the principle of the thing, she admired this beautiful spitfire who was so sure of her rights, and of the inevitable chorus of confirmation she would draw out of her audience. But Devi also found she had less and less to say, and she spent the entire evening quiet, watching. The music throbbed in her head, and she listened to snatches of conversation, words that drifted by and that she recognized, but separate, fragmented, like words in a foreign language she had recently learnt, but still could not put together to make sense.

Devi sat surrounded by people, in increasing isolation, terrified of drawing attention to herself, but aching for any means to do just that.

Hours later, her eyes watering in the smoke-filled room, she remembered she had brought the host an Indian gift, a wall hanging of cotton cloth, hand-printed with vegetable dye. The host held it up for them all to see, and they looked at the blue, baby-faced man on the cloth, bare-chested and crowned with a peacock feather, dancing as he played the flute. For the first time, the image struck Devi as almost grotesque: a grown man, practically naked, wearing a perpetual baby-mask.

'That's Krishna, the dark god who loved milk, butter and women,' said Devi.

'They couldn't bear to have a black god, so they made him blue, huh?' said the intent young woman Devi had earlier admired. She smiled, but her voice was edged with contempt.

Devi laughed with the rest of them, but she knew she had brought the wrong gift. A brass goddess holding a lamp could have been used as an ethnic ashtray. Or safer still, a bottle of wine. It would have been less original, but it would not have set her apart from the others with such finality.

Perhaps Dan had also noticed this dismally insistent separateness that came between them, because he had been unusually quiet as he drove her back home. But what exactly he made of it Devi never guessed, because one month later, close to graduation time, he had asked her to marry him. She saw that this was the logical outcome of the last few months, yet when the question was put to her, she was shocked.

All through her two years of M.A. there had been stray proposals from India, neat little letters from her mother on the bridegroom's prospects, or his parents' reputation for liberalism, making them promising in-laws for a risky oddity, an America-returned bride.

Dan was different. His charm lay in the vast distance they had travelled towards each other, and in Devi's awareness that this distance was not, would not be, completely bridged. This awareness hovered over them like a memory, protective because it remained undiminished.

Devi enjoyed their evenings alone together, and her

enjoyment was necessarily dependent on her inability to conceive of a life with him. Dan was a friend, an experiment for a young woman eager for experience. The possibility of imposing a permanence such as marriage—however flexible in transient America—was somehow obscene.

The innocuous proposals on Indian aerogrammes she had barely read; their world was so distant, so conveniently unfathomable that they failed to move her. She could not find in them a trace of the bridal figure, head bent, forehead radiant, that had been lovingly etched into her mind years ago. The regal, virtuous bride: the image was embedded so deeply that she did not need to open a creaking old cupboard to rediscover the beloved toys of her girlhood.

She had learnt, as most of the 'well-adjusted' foreign students in her university had, to accept the pervading odour of incongruity that shadowed the parallel courses of her Indian and American lives. The unexpected union, the yoking together of dissimilar days and nights, passed off tolerably well as normalcy.

The aerogrammes carried intimations of a different life, woven in gaudy colours that cloaked its own brand of contradictions. But these proposals were not potent enough to reconjure the myth-laden world that had soaked up her past. Instead they led her gently, with grasping, watery fingers, to walk along the shores of an Indian rebirth.

'You are afraid of taking the risk,' said Dan, disappointed in her.

'Going back is a bigger risk. I thought you would see that,' retorted Devi, not sure herself what she meant. But in America you could brazenly plead your rights as an individual.

'What I want to do,' she said, having just thought of it, 'is return to India, maybe for a year, and think it all over.'

'A year is forever,' he protested, but Devi refused to talk about it again.

Since then a kind of equilibrium, unsteady but safe, had hung between them, and Devi began making plans to return. Her mother was delighted, and wrote a long, newsy letter promising a wonderful home-coming, and insisting that she make stopovers at London and Paris to complete her education.

Devi was seized by an eagerness to see these cities she had read so much about, places she had dreamt about for years. Above all, she felt a piercing ache to see her mother. But equally powerful was a nameless dread she only partly acknowledged: the dread of the familiar love, stifling and all-pervasive; of a world beyond her classroom and laboratory, charged with a more pungent uncertainty.

On their last day together, Devi and Dan had planned to see a film in the afternoon, and she had chosen *Casanova*, because she had not seen a film by Fellini before. What she had expected Devi was not sure later, but certainly she was unprepared for the riotous burst of orgiastic copulating, the grotesque hunchback skilfully titillating a balding, ghost-like Casanova. The wine soured in her stomach and knotted her entrails. The monotonous rocking of the bed on the screen tore aside the pastel sheets she had lovingly wrapped the last two weeks in. They now turned into withered, fossil-like ghosts that threatened to come to life in uncontrollable fury. She clutched Dan's hand, warm and mellow, a source of infinite reassurance, and whispered urgently, 'Let's go. Let's go back to your apartment.'

Dan's apartment was on the east side, on the fourteenth floor (the thirteenth actually, but even New Yorkers can be superstitious), overlooking the river. Buried deep in Dan's large leather chair, eyes shut, Devi exorcized Fellini and Casanova, and drank in, gratefully, the soothing jazz Dan had initiated her into.

When she opened her eyes, Dan was watching her, puzzled, but with a quiet respect she immediately responded to. Leaning over, she asked with a sudden surge of affection, 'What is that you are smoking? Grass?'

'Hash.' He paused, then held out the cigarette. 'Would you like to try it? It's good hash, a kind of celebration for our last evening together.'

She had not smoked anything stronger than nicotine before,

but this was something to complete her American experience, a vision of impossibility held at hand's reach, its elusive rays momentarily within her grasp.

She had smoked two, perhaps three joints—she was no longer sure—and her body felt fragile, like a gentle wisp of breeze, floating nameless down a silver-grey, cloudy path, with no end in sight. Every time she closed her eyelids she felt the painful beauty of fireworks without sound, a quiet burst of gold on silver.

Then they were in the water, though she did not quite know how they had got there. She remembered only the jerky lift, and the subway that seemed to go backwards. They raced back, down the tunnel that led to the sea, till the train came to an abrupt halt, and they got out, giggling helplessly.

The windy beach was ice-cold, and the shock of it cleared her head for a minute. 'I've never swum in a sea before,' she said, but Dan didn't hear her. He unpacked a bag of towels and swimming things—he must have packed them then, she thought in surprise—and looked at her with undisguised admiration.

'Exotic bathing beauty,' he said, as if trying out a caption for the hundreds of photographs he took of her. 'I bet you swim like a fish.'

The laughter in her bubbled up again, helping her to forget herself. 'Wait and see,' she shouted, and ran headlong into the murky water.

As she swam stroke after stroke, defying the small waves that crept up to her with frosty fingers, she felt invincible. She was no longer the weak, dog-paddling Devi, a raw, half-baked creature, but someone who had spotted a distant horizon and was swimming towards it.

Then she felt a heavy, iron-like arm clawing her shoulders, pulling her back. She fought desperately, but she was sinking, deeper and deeper into a vast wet grey. She could see neither surface nor muddy floor. In a turbid, breath-choking limbo, she saw herself and Dan, two blurred bodies in struggle, one groping, the other refusing to be weighed down.

He is going to drown, she suddenly thought, and the realization gave her a spurt of vicious strength. Ruthlessly, she pushed him away with her hands, shrugged him off her shoulders, and kicked the desperate hands that finally clung to her legs.

She swam as she had never swum before. The shoreline was only a few minutes away, but she seemed to have lived a spluttering lifetime before the moment when she felt her feet on soft, pliant mud again.

She ran out of the water like a victor, an uncompromising survivor, and took in greedy breathfuls of crisp air. The water streamed down her hair, eyes, nose and ears, but she was warm and flushed with the fact of being alive.

Then she remembered Dan, and as she began screaming for help she felt the frigid evening wind again. It struck her like a hard blow—the oncoming winter, the plane the next day, Dan's big body bobbing up and down the waves.

She spotted two men walking up to the beach and raced towards them. Puffing wetly, trembling with more than the cold, she heard herself shout, 'He's going to drown! He doesn't know how to swim!'

Their pale faces stared at her. They looked at her, a dishevelled, hysterical freak, from a great distance. Then, shrugging their jacket-covered shoulders, they walked on.

The nightmare was beginning all over again. She screamed at their retreating backs till they were out of sight.

Then she raced back to the shore, only to see Dan clambering out of the sea. 'Stop screaming, I'm all right,' he said thickly, and spat out large mouthfuls of muddy water.

Devi woke up in the middle of the night, shivering.

She packed herself tightly in the thick, slippery quilt, but she did not feel warm enough. The same old clouds engulfed her under the quilt.

Something in her was trying to remember: but she couldn't pin any recognizable features on to the memory. Was it something Dan had said? Or some dim memory of an appointment, a quest?

She was not sure, but the faceless memory teased . . . insistent, worrying her for an answer. She pulled herself out of bed and looked for Dan.

She saw instead the beer-bellied, pink-bald, grimy-nailed figure of her New Jersey landlord, heaving his way up the narrow, carpeted stairs to her room. She ran to the door and felt the lock. Her hand firmly holding the lock in place, she leaned against the door with all her weight.

'Come on, come out quickly,' he wheezed outside the door. 'Come and see what I've got for you.'

He pushed against the door, and she ran into her room, looking around frantically. Then she remembered the small knife she kept under her pillow (you must learn to defend yourself in white America, Dan said) and she seized it, and stood erect, ready to spring.

She would plunge it in one quick stroke into his heart. No, no, there would be too much blood. Those arms were what she hated most, blotchy-pink and hairless, spindly and somehow disjointed from the corpulence of his body. They were cunning, not placid like the stomach that heaved in gentle grandfatherly snores as he sat in front of the TV every night. They shot out at odd moments, in odd corners, to stroke her long hair and reach for her breasts, before she could jerk herself free and run up the stairs, three at a time.

She could hear him trying the door. The lock groaned as he twisted the handle outside. Then, as her hand clenched the knife even more tightly, she heard her landlady's car honk as it turned into the driveway.

The clouds were now darker, heavy with barely disguised dangers, and she felt blind, blind, her arms hanging limply, her throat dry, choking all sound out of her, but she screamed. A howl echoed through the darkness and suddenly her arms came back to her mind and she clung to the dark torso near hers. Then the torso grew arms which gripped her firmly and stretched out her racked, feverish body on the bed.

The next day, in the bleak greyness of a morning after, Devi stood alone at the airport, waiting for the plane that would take her thousands of miles closer to home. Her head ached, and her stomach curdled the milk she had drunk. She fought back the nausea that rushed up to her already sour mouth. When the plane was finally ready to take off, there was no one to turn to, and say goodbye. As she ran up to the waiting plane, she felt her American years slip away from her shoulders and trip her up in dank, stagnant puddles around her feet. The brief dream was over. She raced ahead, not so much to escape her purgatory, but to meet halfway, naked and vulnerable, her home-coming.

2

The sun blazes ruthlessly and the sea outside my window is a vast, lustrous mirror, hypnotic and endless. My mother and I live alone in the house by the sea. Our rooms, with identical windows overlooking the beach, are next to each other. Through the wall that separates us, I can hear her humming under her breath as she gets ready for the day. I have never heard her sing before.

Listening, I imagine her, comb in hand, engrossed in a ritual I used to watch with fascination years ago. She would comb out her long, thick hair with firm, brisk strokes till it crackled like something alive. Then she would coil the entire length, her face intent and unsmiling in the mirror. Holding the base of her head with her left hand, she would swiftly, like a magician going through his tricks with ease, twist the coil single-handed, till it became a tight, bulging, spiral shape, like a snake in its mother's womb.

To my surprise, we have seen little of our relatives in Madras. Amma, my mother, Anna, my father, and I had always been a tightly knit little nucleus of our own—I suspect Amma wanted it that way. But in the unusual circumstances, a wandering, only daughter returning to the fold, single, unscathed, her filial piety intact, the practised noses of the extended family would surely twitch with eagerness to ferret out a few hours of entertaining speculation. There would be concern too: though there is enough in the bank for me and my mother to live on, to conduct a decent marriage, I am also their responsibility. A liability, not to be left solely in a widowed mother's hands.

But like a gift to celebrate my home-coming, Amma has kept them all at bay. In this fortress that shuts out the rest of the world, I grope towards her, and she weaves a cocoon, a secure womb that sucks me in and holds me fast to its thick, sticky walls.

There was the initial awkwardness of seeing Amma—unchanged, every hair in place, cool and poised in a silk sari in spite of the sweltering heat. But she was also different; not changed, but less distant, more vulnerable, than the image of her I had carried about with me in America.

In New Jersey, I had wondered at the easy relationships my friends had with their mothers. They chatted about boyfriends, they quarrelled, they kissed. I remember a weekend I spent with my friend, Julie. We were driving back to the campus Sunday evening, and before we left, Julie hugged her mother and said casually, 'I love you, Mom!' I remember my deep embarrassment, as if I had seen an embrace between lovers.

Amma and I did not touch each other and we certainly did not talk about love, for each other or anyone else. But in the first few weeks after my return to Madras, we were intensely conscious of each other; we were pulled together by a tender protectiveness that encircled our necks with its fine threads. Drawn together, my dead father's memory receding for the moment, we became a one-celled unit. We became, not a family, but mother and daughter.

One month later, the honeymoon was over. She had received me with gentleness, even love. In one of those deceptive moments of our reunion, the evening sea breeze as cool and tempting as a fine illusion, I had begun to tell her about America. She smiled gently and said, 'All that is over now. The important thing is that you are back, you are now in Madras. Why go over an old story again?' I had not felt rebuffed then; I had, in fact, been a little flattered that we could speak adult to adult, and that I must have some secrets of my own.

13

We had walked by the seashore every evening in companionable silence, and I was elated by the possibilities of our newly made friendship.

Like a veteran chess player she made her moves. I have to give her credit for her sense of timing. When she had kneaded the dough finely, thoroughly, and I was like putty in her hands, she encircled my shoulders, so ready to lean against her support, and led me to her carefully laid plans—a marriage for me, a *swayamvara*.

The first step was my re-entry into the extended family, a return successfully orchestrated by Amma.

'Devi,' she said one morning, 'will you wear the silk sari I gave you yesterday? You look so thin in these jeans, people will think there is something wrong with you.'

What people, I had wondered, but she suddenly shed that look of waiting on her face. The old Amma I knew so well, decisive, to the point, said to me, 'Everyone is asking to see you, they are wondering why you have become so unsociable. They had better see that you have nothing to hide.'

Everyone was cousins, uncles, aunts. Her brother-in-law, his sisters-in-law, my grandmother's cousin, deaf and frail. They arrived in batches, some for lunch, the less favoured for a quick and steaming-hot coffee.

Amma entertained them all, a picture of dignity and charm, fielding their questions with expert counter-attacks. I, it seemed, was expected to do little. My very presence, the new silk sari, my unforgotten Tamil, the gold chain around my neck, were enough. I sat with them, listened to their news bulletins of births, miscarriages, illnesses and deaths, and answered their probing questions with evasive monosyllables.

The second time around was always easier. They no longer asked me questions; I had only to listen. With her mother's wisdom, Amma proved to them that she had not made a mistake in sending a young, unmarried girl to America. 'Your daughter will be lost to you, Sita'—they had shaken their heads and followed up their prediction with illustrative stories of boys and girls who never came back, married Americans, and forgot their ageing parents in India.

See how I take risks, Amma's look said. She is different, she is special, but she is just as pliant as your home-grown daughters.

Then a cousin of mine, much older than I and now a father of three girls, came visiting. I had always disliked the sly smile that hovered over his double-chinned, sallow face. I ignored him and played with the little girls, who were surprisingly wild and uninhibited. As they ran up and down the stairs, banged doors, screamed to each other from different rooms, my cousin looked at me with an appraising eye.

With the air of an important mission about him, he put on a pair of steel-rimmed glasses and pulled out a sheaf of well-worn papers.

'Here are the horoscopes you wanted,' he said to Amma, who smiled like a beautiful executioner and took them in her hand.

When I turned eighteen, my mother took out my horoscope from a box in her locker. It was stained with auspicious dabs of turmeric-yellow on its four corners, and it smelt faintly of camphor and sandalwood. It seemed already to weave a mysterious spell around us, a web of dark and enchanted ritual.

The horoscope was entrusted to an astrologer, a protégé of my great aunt. I met him soon after. He was a dark, swarthy man with wide, fierce eyes, and a large moustache that seemed to have swallowed most of his mouth. He did not have much use for his mouth anyway; he was mute, surrounded by an impenetrable silence. I stared at him, partly with insolence—I wanted to be contemptuous of all magic-men—and partly overcome by a strange fear of the adulthood, the womanhood that stretched before me.

His eyes held mine in an expressionless gaze for a moment. Then his face and hands came to life and he carved with his gestures in the air the milestones of my life. I would go far away, his right hand indicated, while his eyes scanned the limits of the horizon. His hands turned pages of books, they held them up for his eyes to read. Then his eyes turned sinister, and his hands twirled his moustache.

15

'He is telling us about your husband,' Amma said, and I glared at her. The mute was now rocking a cradle with a grimace that might have been a grotesque imitation of a smile. Then suddenly he brought his hands together in a violent movement, and the thin fingers, tipped by long, grimy nails, mimed the act of breaking, an end of something. All the while his eyes looked at me slyly. Overcome by revulsion, I ran out of the room, seething with hatred.

I thought I had left behind all this charade of obscenities when I travelled far in the next few years. I won a scholarship, and with my parents' encouragement, I set out for America.

Why did I come back? I am not sure. Perhaps it is still too soon for me to understand. But Amma's letters brought with them an unspoken message of loneliness, poignant in its quiet dignity. She has always been a strong, self-willed woman; in my moments of anger I have thought her selfish. But the image of her alone by the sea teased me like a magnet. I saw, over and over again, her small, frail figure, so eloquently upright, the smooth, dark, once-beautiful face now devoid of that circle of red on her forehead that completed the vision of wife, mother. I heard the low, modulated voice, at once commanding and coaxing. I never dreamt of her as I did of my father, craving for a means to get closer to him. But she was always our anchor-rock, never wrong, never to be questioned, a self-evident fact of our existence. That she might need me, my hesitant, self-doubting presence, was intoxicating.

Her hand seemed to turn me away from the indecisive confusion of my last months in America; she seemed to have silently articulated the pattern she had perceived in the jigsaw puzzle that confronted me.

With the same eloquent hand, my mother prepared me for my *swayamvara*. When I was adept at wearing the right jewels and sari, the right smile; when I made the naïve and therefore innocent small talk suitable for a marriageable girl among her elders; when she had fed and stoked the rapidly returning memories of my grandmother's stories of predestined husbands and idyllic marriages, Amma played her next card.

She invited the Srinivasans to meet me, view me as a potential bride. The parents came without their son, since it was only a preliminary visit. They were urbane, sophisticated—let's be friends, no formalities please, they said. He was an economist, highly regarded in a UN organization. She had taught political science in a women's college for years. They were always going away to Europe, Africa, three years in each place on deputation. Their son, a scientist in Bombay, had won several gold medals in the course of his studies. He lives and breathes pure physics, they said. He wants a Brahmin wife, they said with visible pride.

'All this is just for show,' the mother said to me, as if we had known each other for years, indicating with a manicured hand her short, dyed hair. 'Scratch my skin and you'll find a south Indian. A good, south Indian Brahmin.'

So they were looking for an accomplished bride, a young woman who would talk intelligently to her scientist husband's friends, but who would also be, as all the matrimonial ads in the Sunday papers demanded, fair, beautiful, home-loving and prepared to 'adjust'.

When they left, I turned to Amma, furious. Even as she silenced my indignation with cajoling reassurance, I saw a new, unfamiliar weariness on her face.

'I suppose I will have to tell them when they call me tomorrow,' she said. 'It's embarrassing, Dr Srinivasan was very kind to your father and me in Africa. But it's all for the best. We can't be too cautious when choosing a husband.'

The Madras sun wrung sweat out of every pore in my body. But I welcomed the heat, the stillness, the warm blanket thrown over all the questions in my mind. The afternoons I had spent with my grandmother, many many summers ago, had the same quality of warm reassurance.

Her home, a small dilapidated house in the *agraharam*, was full of mysteries, even dangers, for a six-year-old girl. I remember the day a large lizard leapt on my bare leg as I sat watching her in the *puja* room. I screamed again and again, as I felt the lizard, cold and

17

clammy against my flesh. I knew, somehow, that this was like death; like the dark coldness of the old cow foaming at the mouth, eyes vapid after a night of moaning and mournful mooing that reached the house from the cowshed in the backyard.

My grandmother's lap was soft, and she murmured gently like a little brown and yellow bird, but the bony thighs I felt through her soft sari were as warm and solid as the afternoon-baked earth below me. Her *pallav* covered my face, enclosing it, a silken refuge.

Through the long, still summers of my childhood, my grandmother laid out for me the feast of a bride's choice, the regal dignity and solemnity of a *swayamvara*.

'Let me tell you how the beautiful princess Damayanti got married,' she said one afternoon, as she peeled little portions of jackfruit and put them in my mouth. The cloying, sick-sweet smell turned my stomach, but she had taught me the pleasure of biting into this thick, succulent flesh.

'Listen,' she said. 'The morning of the *swayamvara*, the sun shone more brightly than usual.'

('Why?' I asked.

'Because the sun knows where it's getting its light from,' she said.)

'The sun's golden rays were reflected in the polished brass columns of the amphitheatre. A long procession of kings, princes and gods entered its lofty portals, and each was received by a nymph-like maiden who led him to a throne bearing the sceptre and turban of his state.'

('What's a nymph?' I asked.

'A woman who is very beautiful and never has children,' she said. 'That's why she always remains a girl.')

'All the kings were dressed in robes and jewels of such brilliance, the eye did not know where to look. And the gods—oh, they were dazzling! They did not sweat, even in their heavy robes of brocaded silk, and their feet did not quite touch the ground.'

('How did they walk then?' I asked.

'They didn't need to. They were carried; or they simply floated.'

'But why didn't they touch the ground?'

'Because they were only there for the girl. They didn't want to dirty their feet with our dust and grime. Now listen. Damayanti is about to come in.')

'Damayanti entered the hall with an escort, trumpets blaring, and a secret glow of promise surrounded her face and hands, and the garland of sweet-smelling jasmines and roses she held.'

('Why was it a secret promise?' I asked, forgetting to keep quiet.

'Everything about a bride is a secret,' she said, forgetting to scold me for interrupting her again.)

'Earlier Damayanti had been anointed by her maids with fragrant oils and a paste of rice powder, turmeric and sandalwood. Slim-waisted jars encrusted with precious stones were lifted over her head. The fresh spring water flowed over her and then her fair body was dried with silk. Her hair braided with pearls and emeralds, her eyes darkened with kohl, a vermilion circle glowing in the centre of her forehead, she floated like a fresh lotus down the carpets of the hall.'

('Will I be fair like Damayanti when I grow up?'

'Of course you will. I'll rub you down with coconut oil and turmeric till you are a pale, pale princess.')

'Not a sound was heard in the hall as the kings held their breath and Damáyanti walked slowly, surely, towards the row of enthroned bridegrooms-to-be. She would stop occasionally, in front of one of the thrones, and the silence would give way to a song in praise of the king she beheld, sung by his own minstrels.

The heralds of the princess issued their challenge in verse, witty and brief; and the kings' heralds would reply, in defence of their masters' achievements and virtue. But Damayanti listened with only one ear. Her heart, loyal and steadfast, never wavered from the path leading to Nala, the king of the Nishadas, and her feet, adorned with gold rings and henna, were sure of their destination. The honeyed words of Nala's courier, the wild swan who had won her heart for him, sang in her ear as she sought out her destiny.'

('But why did she pretend to listen to the other kings?'
'Because a woman gets her heart's desire by great cunning.')

In my grandmother's stories, there was room only for heroes and heroines. Princesses grew up secure in the knowledge of what awaited them: love, a prince who was never short of noble, and a happy ending. No question, however fine and niggling, took my grandmother by surprise. She twisted it, turned it inside out, and cooked up her own home-made yardsticks for life.

'You too will live like a princess,' she would say fondly to me between her kisses, and I listened, rapt, my seven-year-old mind thrilling at the splendours that awaited me.

I am glad my grandmother is no longer alive. I am glad she is not here to see me at my *swayamvara*, the princess' robe she lovingly stitched for me frayed round the edges and two sizes too large.

I am glad she cannot see the gift package Dan has sent me across the seas. A green shirt with straps instead of sleeves, a bright yellow palm tree splashed on its front. Sun and sand, it declares in a bold yellow, celebrating the joys of a warm winter in Madras.

Between interviews with bridegrooms, my womanly modesty protected by six yards of silk, I steal into my room with the package. I spread out the shirt and the swimsuit with the plunging neckline on my bed, and gaze at them wonderingly as if they are relics I cannot place in time. I roll up the fine, soft synthetic in my hands and bury my nose in it, as if I can smell out a clue, some connection which would link these two obstinately disparate chapters of my life.

I must have met five, no six prospective bridegrooms in three months. One, more enterprising than the rest, insisted on an evening out at a five-star hotel. He was quite adept at the game of choosing a bride. All through dinner (earlier he sent back our chocolate milk shakes because the milk had turned), he drew me out expertly, asking me the most searching questions in the middle of small talk. I leaned back—this was not so bad after all—and slowly I found myself telling him about Dan. Actually Dan has receded into the past quite gracefully; he has slipped through my fingers and left no scar. I found I could talk about him easily, and with the affection born of nostalgia for a safely closed chapter. The bridegroom-gentleman listened politely, and helped me along with an understanding devoid of prurient interest. He suggested we dance, and in his formal arms I danced a waltz I did not know, eyes shut, willing myself to slip into a day-dream about life as his lover, his wife. When he dropped me back, at the sensible hour of 10 p.m., I smiled at him with genuine fondness.

The next morning I woke up late, with a mild tremor of anticipation. But Amma met my looks without a smile. Looking at her inscrutable eyes, I remembered that she would never resort to the kindness of white lies or procrastination. She announced, as if I had asked her, that I was not quite what the young man had in mind. I was not disappointed, but surprised; and looking at her, also a little guilty. I could see her set smile, giving away nothing, as she fended off curious old aunts on their next visit.

The next day was a day for visions; for ghosts. It was dark and rainy, and huge, sullen clouds hung over the sea, turning it into an awesome stranger. The mute I had thought long dead (but he was only a young man then, I realized with shock), sat at Amma's feet awaiting me.

I hesitated, but I was no longer a child susceptible to the power of magic; and I turned to Amma, saying, 'Is this necessary?'

She did not reply, and I turned back to the mute, bracing

21

myself for the horror-show of a weird mime-dance, a travesty of the romantic gypsy with her crystal ball. But he too had read the need of the moment. His hands lay still on a pile of horoscopes and he stared at me, a long piercing stare that had lost little of the hypnotic power of his youth, but which was now tempered with a message of reconciliation, perhaps resignation.

Later in the evening, the sky cleared unexpectedly, and the beach was cloaked with a moist freshness. The wind that had roared a few hours earlier had dissipated itself, and a benign breeze invited the merriment of the evening crowd of children playing on the sands, their bare feet leaving clear marks on the deep brown mud.

A week later, lulled by the music in the air, the ripples of promise in the sea, I met and accepted Mahesh. I had the limpid-eyed blessings of my mother, and I never saw the mute again.

Mahesh, the stranger who is to be my husband, visits us for an hour every evening. He is no prince, but a regional manager in a multinational company that makes detergents and toothpaste.

'I travel a great deal,' he tells me, as we sit on the sand, a couple, like the other pairs who dot the evening seashore. But we don't look at each other furtively as some of the others do, their hands crawling across the sand like secretive crabs and colliding innocently.

'I will be in Bangalore only ten days of the month,' Mahesh says. 'Are you ready to accept that? My father is there, of course, and our old maidservant, but you will be lonely sometimes. Have you thought of that?'

I had. If I was going to be left alone a little, I thought, I could get used to it all. Slowly, without the labels of wife and daughter-in-law branded on me the first day, a twenty-four hour, thirty days a month job.

And I liked Mahesh's frankness, his willingness to be fair, even if he did seem to be an unbending pillar of propriety and good sense. He is honest at least, I thought, he admits to wanting a woman at home who will be a wife and a mother. Some of the others I had met had amazed me with their pretence that they were not shopping for a wife. They had chatted and charmed, grilled me about America. While they looked into my eyes amorously, as if we had met for a romantic purpose, they sneaked out questions about what food I liked to cook and how many children I wanted to have.

If I was going to play out a travesty of the myths that had filled my childhood, I would tear aside all pretence, I thought, I would be as matter-of-fact as Mahesh.

Mahesh returned to Bangalore, and my mother summoned the family to begin the hectic and long-drawn preparation for the wedding. She hired two cooks and rented a large house for a month, so that all the guests would be well looked after with home-cooked food. I don't want my house and garden to get filthy, she said to me, and we moved to the house that had seen so many weddings, its storeroom now overflowing with coconuts, rice and jaggery.

The relatives began to arrive, four or five a day, and the house filled up. Children ran between the mattresses that lined the floors and dodged their scolding mothers. The women held small conferences about saris, the flowers to be bought, the invitation cards to be handed to the guests personally, during visits that would stretch over weeks. Amma let them have their say. She offended no one, listened to every bit of advice as if she had never heard it before, then did exactly what she wanted. The men detached themselves elegantly from the bustle, and sat talking all day under the droning fans in the front room, till one or the other was called upon to escort the women on yet another invitation-giving or shopping trip.

To my deep relief, they were all so busy that they left the bride alone. Every time I ventured out of my room, someone would pat me and say, Don't worry, don't worry. It will all be over soon, and you will be settled. What a lucky girl you are!

Between the long, loud meals and the sessions of inspecting

Githa Hariharan

saris and jewels, I sat in my room, alone. I sat at my desk, trying to write to friends about the wedding next month, my wedding. Letters to explain the turn of my life, explanations I half-heartedly attempted, even as my pen met the festive letter-paper.

24

3

As a child I spent every summer in my grandmother's house in the village.

My grandmother was a wizened old woman, illiterate, and widowed in her early thirties. She was as thin as a stick. Her shoulder-length, lank grey hair was tied in a never-changing knot about the size of a large gooseberry. The most noticeable feature of her long, bony face was her shiny buck-teeth; she had her own teeth till she died. But her face was also lit up by her brown, tapering eyes. They could have been called beautiful once, I suppose, but what made them alive was a trick she had of moving her eyeballs quickly, side to side, like a Bharata Natyam dancer wound up to perform in fast motion. As a child I often tried to imitate this rapid movement, which became almost frenzied when she told me her goriest stories. But I could never do it right, though I practised for hours in front of the mirror.

I don't think she had ever seen herself in the mirror. She was totally devoid of any physical vanity. The only thing I saw her wear was a faded nine-yard sari draped between her legs so that she did not need a petticoat underneath. She never wore a blouse—modern nonsense, she called it—and challenged my disapproving mother in a sudden, unexpected moment of aggression: What do I have to hide?

So her breasts, two elongated, dry brown raisins, the large

nipples not far from the navel, were covered only by the top half of her sari. They were almost as familiar to me as her face.

Every summer she would wait for us in the old stone porch outside her house, squinting, as our car drove down the dirt-track road, raising clouds of dust.

She would weep unashamed tears when she saw me and lift me out of the car, as if I was a baby. She never let us in till she had exorcized the ghosts clinging to us from our other life in the city. She would quickly fetch a bowl of water mixed with turmeric, and we had to stand by the doorway as she drew large circles in the air with the bowl in her hands. Then she emptied the yellowing water in the street, and ushered us in. Our summer began with this auspicious welcome, the three of us cleansed of all impurities.

Thus we lived ordinary lives most of the year, in a house Amma filled with her mottoes, the words I heard most often from her as I was growing up: order, reason, progress. But every summer, we lived another life with my grandmother.

My grandmother's domain, the ritual in which she encased our arrivals and departures, our visits to relatives or the village temple, was more ambiguous. It was also richer, irresistible, and through her I fell in love with the god-like heroes and heroines whose stories were as real, more real, to her than our own.

It occurs to me now that there couldn't have been more than five or six people in her household during our annual visits. But after our large, silent house in Madras, where nobody would have guessed a small child lived, my grandmother's little house, stuck to similar houses on either side, seemed to throb with life.

Her maidservant Gauri's domestic problems were discussed as if they were our own. Distant relatives who had been orphaned, or deserted by philandering husbands, found in her house a warm refuge. They came and went, and my grandmother never let them go empty-handed. She was one of the worst cooks I have ever met, but she was always doling out generous helpings of her messes to grateful destitutes. One impoverished widow, a great aunt, was sent away with a large, overflowing tiffin carrier, three saris and enough vegetables for a month. Another, a young woman whose husband and father-in-law ill-treated her in turns, was reassured with advice culled from the epics. In my grandmother's home, I didn't need a window to look at a mysterious, unknown world outside.

And most of all, in my memories of those summers, my grandmother's house is crowded with superhuman warriors, men and women destined to lead heroic lives. For many summers, I thrived on a diet of her caressing gnarled fingers and her stories of golden splendour.

'Listen, my child,' she would begin, her hand unravelling the stray knots in my wet hair, 'listen to these stories of men and women who loved, shed blood, and met their deaths as ardently as they lived.'

My grandmother's stories were no ordinary bedtime stories. She chose each for a particular occasion, a story in reply to each of my childish questions. She had an answer for every question. But her answers were not simple: they had to be decoded. A comparison had to be made, an illustration discovered, and a moral drawn out. Like the sugar shapes she made for me, a rich, over-sweet syrup that was magically transformed over the fire into ornamented little elephants, swans with each feather delicately etched, her stories fashioned moulds. Ideal moulds, impossibly ambitious, that challenged the puny listener to stretch her frame and fit into the vast spaces, live up to her illustrious ancestors.

I remember the time I found an old photo of Amma's. It was a studio photograph of her alone, the kind that is still sent, but now in real life colours, to prospective bridegrooms by the girl's family. Amma did not look like herself. Her eyes had a vague, dreamy look about them, softening the chin that already jutted out a little, like a portent of her later determination. What surprised me even more was that she held a veena in her hands, her fingers caressing the strings.

I wonder now what Amma would have said if I had taken the photograph to her. I didn't, I went to my grandmother instead.

'Pati,' I said, wriggling my way on to her lap where I was always welcome, 'did Amma play the veena when she was a girl?'

'Where did you find that photo?' she said. 'I thought your mother had torn them all.' Then that look I knew so well, that exalted story-look, crossed her face and she asked, 'Do you know about Gandhari, my little one? Listen; listen and you will learn what it is to be a real woman.'

'When Gandhari came to her husband's house, dressed in her bridal finery, her heart beat like a drum as she was led through the marble palace to the bridegroom-prince's chamber.'

('Why didn't he come out to welcome her?'
'It's only in the silly stories you read in books that princes look for princesses. Actually it's the other way round.')

'The palace Gandhari was now to rule as queen was twice as big, twice as magnificent as her parents' palace. Priceless gems, the size of ripe pumpkins, hung at the tips of chandeliers; the marble pillars shone like mirrors. Four sentries at the prince's door bowed low as she approached them, her hands fluttering amid her attendants' warm, clasping fingers.

'The huge wooden doors opened slowly, and Gandhari's eager eyes lost their shyness as she sought those of her new husband. His sentries, her attendants, stood by, pillar-like, but with faces that brimmed over with a breathless anticipation. Many years later, when she had learnt the hard lesson that the splendid palace lacked only one luxury—privacy—she would grasp the significance of the twitching lips, the curiosity-filled eyes of her witnesses.'

('But why didn't they tell her?'
'Because, my child, a woman meets her fate alone.')

'Gandhari brushed aside the maid closest to her and walked to her husband with quick, impatient steps. He stood by the window, his noble head looking up at the sky. But when he turned around, she saw the white eyes, the pupils glazed and useless.'

('If he was so noble, why did he agree to marry her?'
    'All husbands are noble, Devi. Even the blind and deaf ones.')

'In her pride, her anger, Gandhari said nothing. But she tore off a piece of her thick red skirt and tied it tightly over her own eyes. She groped towards her unseeing husband, her lips straight and thin with fury.

'Gandhari was not just another wilful, proud woman,' said my grandmother, summing up. 'She embraced her destiny—a blind husband—with a self-sacrifice worthy of her royal blood.'

I said nothing, and was not precocious enough to ask how Gandhari's story and Amma's came together. Or perhaps I knew. I must have known, even then, that Gandhari's pride, the fury that was to become her life-force, the central motive of years of blind suffering, was no piece of fiction. Gandhari's anger, wrapped tightly round her head in a life-long blindfold, burnt in a heart close, very close to mine.

The anger of the gods, I had learnt, is unpredictable: it is also inevitable. Divine anger provides those twists and turns in mortal destinies that make heroism possible. The lesson that was more difficult to digest was human anger: that it could seep into every pore of a womanly body and become the very bloodstream of her life.

I listened to my grandmother's interpretation of Gandhari's choice, but the lesson I learnt was different. The lesson brought me five steps closer to adulthood. I saw, for the first time, that my parents too were afflicted by a kind of blindness. In their blinkered world they would always be one, one leading the other, one hand always in the grasp of another.

Through the circuitous route all her journeys took, my grandmother finally came back to Amma's photograph.

'When your mother was a young bride,' she said to me, 'she

brought to my house a veena that she had inherited as part of her dowry. Her parents had heard her talent even as a little child and had trained her with the best teacher they could find.

'She played so beautifully, our household came to a standstill as the tears streamed down our faces. Through the wetness, your father's eyes shone with pride as they settled on that head bent over the veena, lost in concentration. She had been trained as a daughter-in-law too, of course, and she played the veena every day after she had finished her household duties.

'Then one day, my husband sat in front of the gods, ready for his morning prayers. He couldn't find a thing he needed. The flowers had not been picked, the floor had not been swept. "Sita," he called, his voice trembling with anger. She did not hear him, but from her room we heard the sound of the veena in rapturous flight.

'I put down my knife in the kitchen and hurried to her room. But he got there first, and I heard him roar, "Put that veena away. Are you a wife, a daughter-in-law?"

'Sita hung her head over the veena for a minute that seemed to stretch for ages, enveloping us in an unbearable silence. Then she reached for the strings of her precious veena and pulled them out of the wooden base. They came apart with a discordant twang of protest.

'She looked up at my husband, her eyes dry and narrowed, and said in a clear, stinging whisper, "Yes. I am a wife, a daughter-in-law."

'We never saw her touch the veena again. She became a dutiful daughter-in-law the neighbours praised, and our household never heard that heart-rending music again.'

In my grandmother's mind, the link between her stories and our own lives was a very vital one. But she could not always find a precise mythological equivalent for the puzzling experiences the people we knew had. The lesser lives we knew did not always rise to the heroic proportions of my mother's version of Gandhari's sacrifice.

I must have, as I grew older, begun to see the fine cracks in the bridge my grandmother built between the stories I loved, and the less self-contained, more sordid stories I saw unfolding around me. The cracks I now see are no longer fine, they gape as if the glue that held them together was counterfeit in the first place. But the gap I now see is also a debt: I have to repair it to vindicate my beloved storyteller.

In my grandmother's house, I sat by the well every week, a sari draped across the clothes-line like a curtain, so that her maidservant, Gauri, could massage me for hours with warm coconut oil. She smelt earthy sweet, like some ripe fruit sweating in the midday sun.

'Do you eat goats and pigs, Gauri?' I asked her one day and she chuckled with delight.

'Where is the money, little one? On the day you get married, I will kill a nice, fat, juicy goat and offer it to the godd⌐ ⌐s.'

She was a young woman as golden-skinned as her name, and when she walked home from the pond, freshly bathed, her dripping clothes covered with a plain white sari, she looked, I thought, like a river goddess.

Gauri had worked in the Brahmin houses as long as she could remember. As long as she could remember, she had been working to build a little pile of dowry-gold, chain by chain, bangle by bangle.

'They ask for fifty sovereigns of gold, Amma,' she said to my grandmother. 'And after ten years of work I have only fifteen. There is still the nose-stud to be bought, the toe-rings, the stone earrings set in gold, and the *thali*.'

'But Gauri is so beautiful, she could have a *swayamvara*,' I said to my grandmother that night.

'She will get married soon, Devi. You wait and see,' she comforted me. The next year, when I came to my grandmother's house for the summer, Gauri ran in to tell us the news. The wedding was only a week away. He came from a big family, but she was used to hard work.

'How many sovereigns?' my grandmother asked, interrupting her. Gauri stared at her feet awkwardly.

'Twenty, Amma. But I have almost eighteen. I'll get the rest

31

somehow.'

I danced round Gauri and begged to see the wedding. My grandmother and Gauri began to laugh, all their adult seriousness about gold forgotten.

'Just this once, Pati,' I wheedled, my little finger expertly twisting about my grandmother's sweet grey head.

I dressed with as much care as the bride, and with a maidservant on either side, I went to Gauri's wedding. The drums and the nadaswaram at the entrance of the thatched hut went mad in joyful disharmony, but no one noticed their noise. People screamed to each other over the blaring music, and when Gauri appeared, radiant in her hard-won gold, the drums split our ears with their unruly tumult.

I gave her Pati's gift, my lips trembling with excitement. Long after the maidservants took me home, we heard the distant sounds of revelry, a voice raised in song, and the clamorous drumbeat, on and on.

Gauri came to see Pati some years later, to ask if she could have her old job back. Her husband was an animal, she said. They treated her like dirt, she said. But Pati had already heard several stories from the servants. She had heard that Gauri had fallen in love with her young brother-in-law. He sat at home all day with the women instead of going to work. He was afraid of the shocked stares he got when he stepped out of their hut. He was tall, slim, almost handsome. But his arms, face, neck, as far as the eye could see above the closely buttoned shirt, were a riotous orgy of coral-pink maps. Like an acid river, the leucoderma spread across his body, making him an outcaste. And Gauri had fallen in love with this albino-turning freak, whom nature in her capriciousness had made a tender, steadfast lover. They plotted behind the elders' backs and ran away one night. She even took with her ten of the gold sovereigns, now chains around her neck and bangles on her arms, a proud and unrepentant housewife.

Pati would not give her work to do in the house again, but she sent her away with a ten-rupee note. That night, she sat by my bed, unusually quiet, with a kind of hurt bewilderment.

'Tell me about the *Mahabharatam*, Pati,' I said.

'No, not today, Devi. But I will tell you about the beautiful girl who married a snake.'

'A good, simple woman and her husband longed for a child. If you don't have a child, you displease the gods; if the gods are angry, they make sure you don't have a child.'

('They are always angry then. It's their fault the couple didn't have a child!'

'Now that you are a big ten-year-old girl, Devi, remember this: it's never their fault. It's always ours.')

'So the childless couple offered the gods a series of austere sacrifices. Their prayers were answered, and a little black snake was born to the woman. Her neighbours screamed when they saw the hooded infant in the cradle, but she sent them away, and fed the snake at her breast.'

('How horrible! Did the snake bite her?'

'Snakes don't have teeth; they have fangs. And when you are a mother, you'll see: your child's bite will be just like a kiss.')

'Then, when the snake grew into adulthood, fifteen feet of sinuous coils, she streaked its hood with auspicious vermilion and turmeric, and asked her husband to find her a good daughter-in-law. He railed at her foolishness, but she stood before him, her hands on her hips, eyes blazing with a mother's righteous wrath.

'The husband packed his bundle and walked to distant lands. He said to his hosts, "I travel in search of a wife fit for my son." Now the host had a very beautiful daughter, and so he said, "Take her for your own."

'When his neighbours saw him return with the fair beauty and her attendants, they cried, "Will this pearl-like maiden marry that venom-tongued snake?"

'But the young bride lifted her veil and said, "A girl is given only once in marriage. So stop this mockery of lamenting and wailing. Let me go to my waiting husband."

33

'Then she married him, and was a devoted wife, looking after all his needs.

('She *liked* snakes?'
'She liked this one. She married him, didn't she?')

'One night, the serpent slithered out of the chest in her chamber and crawled into her bed. When she clasped her arms about him, she felt the scales soften underneath her hands till they touched tender human flesh. She embraced the good fortune she had brought about with her loving hands, and they spent a night of warm caresses. Towards dawn, the young woman slipped out of her husband's embrace and got out of the bed. On the floor she saw yards of cold snake-skin ripped apart in the middle. She quickly dragged the skin outside and burnt it to ashes. Then she went back to her bed, where the sweet-smelling youth slept on, unaware of his rebirth.'

I remember I spent days trying to unravel this message from my grandmother. Should Gauri, my happy, down-to-earth Gauri, have married a snake? And who was the snake in her story—her bestial husband or her freakish lover?

Every time I saw Gauri after that—she was loyal and never forgot us, coming to see me every summer—I was filled with a sense of foreboding. Gauri seemed her usual cheerful self; I could see no scars, detect no signs of turbulence. But I still longed to give her some clue, a hint that would enable her to penetrate the snake-skin that spread itself between her and feminine fulfilment.

As my grandmother grew older, her shoulders, always frail, began to hunch a little. She stooped, as if under a heavy burden. Her bent back suddenly seemed vulnerable, so that she now looked like the other old women in the village, left behind by their families, to wait in the midst of what they had known all their lives. She, like them, was waiting to die.

Whether it was this new oldness, a grey frailty that did not match the vivid colours she still spoke of, or whether she thought I was old enough, I am not sure. But my grandmother's stories began around this time to take on a sharper, more precarious tone of dangerous possibilities. I remember how I first heard about Amba, the princess who shed her womanhood through her dreams of revenge and became a man; I remember that it was Uma's story that inspired my grandmother to talk to me about Amba.

When my cousin Uma got married, every corner of the house was scrubbed till the floor was a new, unfamiliar colour, and the wide balconies where I played hopscotch were covered with intricate yellow and white *kolams*. I wore a new skirt, long and delicate, with paisley designs in gold along its edge, and bangles on my arms and flowers in my short but tightly plaited hair.

In the afternoon, I stole up to Uma's newly allotted room, I no longer remember why. Uma and her husband were alone, and around them lay open the suitcases she was packing to take away with her. I lingered round the doorway, unnoticed, and before I could decide what to do next, he grasped her hand, and a look passed between them, some kind of a signal I could not read, and I ran down the stairs, breathless, ashamed, and oppressed by a kind of excitement.

A year later, I must have been fourteen or fifteen then, Uma returned and lived with my grandmother till the old woman died. The monsoons had just begun when Uma returned, and the next few months people came and went in the rain, and everything was damp, limp, full of murmured secrets. A few months later, I heard Uma's story: a motherless girl like her was lucky to have found a match in a wealthy home, or so everybody thought. Her husband and his father drank till she was stupefied with fear; even her girlhood, spent with an indifferent father and a hostile stepmother, had not prepared her for this trial. Her foreboding grew into terror when her drunken father-in-law kissed her roughly on the lips.

I must have pestered my grandmother with questions about Uma and her brief marriage, because she began telling me often that I was the *devi* of our house, and that I would be treated as a goddess of good fortune wherever I went. It strikes me now that her face was touched by a sadness when she said that, sadness and perhaps a shadow of uncertainty.

'Ah, Devi,' she said, 'why weep over Uma? A high-born prince, or even a goddess, has been the victim of disaster. But a woman like Amba, a truly courageous woman, finds the means to transform her hatred, the fate that overtakes her, into a triumph.

'Listen. When the noble Bheeshma, born of a goddess, went to Kashi, he heard of a *swayamvara* being held at the palace. Three beautiful princesses, Amba, Ambika and Ambalika, were to choose husbands from the crowds of princes and kings gathered together that fateful morning.

'His vow of celibacy pricked Bheeshma like an old scar that flares at the touch of a teasing flame. But the noble mind has answers for almost everything. He remembered his young stepbrother, and walked into the *swayamvara* hall, a latecomer who swaggered in with the confidence of a winner. He saw the three princesses wafting across to the kings like a silver ribbon, uncreased and virginal. Amba, the eldest, led the princesses, and held out her garland to the young king of Salwa. The jasmines had barely brushed the princely neck, when the air was filled with piercing screams, trampling feet and clouds of dust. Rough hands seized Amba. Before she could turn around to see who had interrupted her heart's destiny, she heard her sisters' cries, and felt the bumping of swift chariot wheels below her.'

('Why didn't Amba's father stop him? Or Salwa? Or anyone else?'
    'Once he had laid his manly hands on her shoulders, Devi, she was no longer a girl. A woman fights her battles alone.')

'Bheeshma's face shone with pride as he presented his booty to his stepmother, the queen of the Kurus. She embraced the princesses, calling them her daughters-in-law. Amba held the queen's hands tightly in hers, and in a soft and pleading voice confided her secret. Her heart had been given away, her garland had almost encircled the neck of the man she had chosen.

'Could a pure princess give her heart to two men without bringing shame to her unborn sons?'

('But she was kidnapped! She didn't have to give her heart to him.'

'When you marry, Devi, your heart moves up to your shoulder and slips down your arm to the palm of your hand. The hand that holds yours tightly as you walk round the fire receives it like a gift. You can't do anything about it: when you marry, it goes to him and you never get it back.')

'Bheeshma and his stepmother were speechless with surprise. But they quickly recovered their royal poise. So what if one-third of the booty were lost? The other two were young, they would bear the royal house strong warrior-sons.

' "Go, Amba," said Bheeshma, "go where you will. Be a faithful wife to the man you have chosen."

'Amba bade her sisters goodbye and set out for her lover's palace in Salwa. She strung garlands of jasmine on the way, two fragrant flowers for each that had earlier been so rudely snatched away from her hands.

'She walked with a bride's grace up to Salwa's throne. "I am here, O King," she said for all the court to hear, "to keep the promise I almost made earlier. You are my chosen husband. See the wife who stands before you, pure and untouched as her garland of fresh flowers."

'Salwa roared with crude, mirthless laughter. His face twisting with rage, he said, "Do you think I feast on leftovers? I am a king. I do not touch what another man has won in battle. Go to Bheeshma. He won you when his arrow struck my eager hands on your luckless garland. He is your husband. What have you to do with me?"

'Even when she had been kidnapped from her father's palace, Amba had not felt as orphaned as she did now. She crept back, shrunken in her bridal robes, to Bheeshma's palace. She waited at the door of his bedchamber, her face wreathed in the shadows of the oncoming night.'

Githa Hariharan

('Why didn't she go back home?'

'A woman without a husband has no home.')

'When Bheeshma had put away his armour of courtly robes, she ran in and shut the door behind her. "Take me for your wife, Bheeshma," she wept. She tore her frail veils aside.

"Look at me, Bheeshma. See my face, trembling with eagerness. See my breasts, full and ready. See my arms, my legs, gentle and soft as the most tender and clinging of creepers. See my womanhood that longs to be fulfilled. Will you look away? Will you put a selfish vow made in the foolishness of youth before the desperate offering I make you?"

'Bheeshma trembled with desire, but he had spent his youth building thick walls of masculine deafness around himself. The echo that sent a tremor along his spine was, however moving, muffled. He sent Amba away, his face safely averted.'

('But why? I know he liked her. Didn't he carry her away in his chariot?'

'He was a brave man, so he couldn't be a loser at the *swayamvara*. Later, he remembered the vow that made him more of a god and less of a man. And anyway: Amba punished him for his brief spell of manhood.')

'The young princess had lived several lifetimes in a week or two. She cast aside her finery, the trappings of a life denied to her, and set out for the forest, a new hardness in her heart. She no longer thought of silks, thrones, flowers, children; she had thrown away her woman's lot when Bheeshma scorned her offering. Now she was a woman only in name.

'The hardness that congealed into hatred was the child of the men who had spurned her. She nurtured this sweet poison till it fed her, quenched her voracious thirst, and clothed the body that took pleasure in every form of mortification.

'Lost in her insatiable desire for revenge, Amba spent long years in the forest, with her hatred as a faithful companion. It lit her way through the darkest, coldest night, and slithered round her muddy, gravelly locks, deadlier than the man-feared snake.

'When she had, with superhuman energy, piled penance on penance; poured the bitter juices from her hard nipples as libation for the hissing fires; lit a fire so powerful within her that the forest night groaned with the festering wound in its bosom, Amba stood ready to meet Shiva, a garland of thick-skinned, flesh coloured *nagalinga pushpa* in her hands.

'Shiva saw the desire leap into her eyes; he knew what she strained towards. He took the garland from her, gently, so gently, because those fingers razed to ashes anything they touched, and promised Amba her revenge. Whoever wears this garland will surely kill Bheeshma, he said.

'Then Amba travelled to the courts of many kings famed for their valour, and offered them her garland of destruction. But not one dared to fight Bheeshma, not even with Shiva's weapon around his neck. Would Amba never learn? She threw the garland around a pillar in King Drupada's court and stormed out, to meet the death she had so long been marked for. She died alone in the forest, her heart, what was left of it, broken into rocky little splinters.

'But the hooded flowers she had cradled in her bosom, the child of her all-consuming hatred, lived on. Amba was reborn as Drupada's daughter, a daughter raised as a son.'

('Why?'
    'Can a daughter raised as a daughter become a man?')

'So when the time was ripe, she became a man, and with the garland of Amba round his neck, he rode the plains of Kurukshetra to taste the heady sweetness of the beloved's blood in battle.'

Did my grandmother know what she was saying? On the threshold of senility for years—she collected in her old age more and more wounded refugees in her house, stray objects of charity—her stories reached a frenzied pitch of fantasy. Close to death, she made me a gift of the ultimate fantasy: a woman avenger who could earn

manhood through her penance. The difference between Amba, and
a mere mortal, a woman like Uma, lay in the strength to seize
sorrow and uncertainty, and pour the mixture into the sieve of her
penance. Whatever emerged, however bloody and vengeful, was
a distilled potion of good fortune. No heroine died without this
powerful and destructive protest that left its mark, a memorial to
a fighter, behind her.

I was terrified by Uma's marriage, but I was also terrified by
the vengeful Amba.

Amba's story, or maybe it was Uma's, made a deep impression
on me, like an irresistible horror-film, and I day-dreamed more and
more about female avengers.

Summer after summer with my grandmother, I had learnt
firsthand the all-pervading power of the gods and goddesses.

One or the other watches your every step, I heard. An assistant
goddess keeps records of every mortal on lotus leaves with a pen
of reeds. To be noticed by the gods, however, to be singled out for
an encounter, you have to be a heroine or a villainess. Or beautiful.
I was not, my arms and legs stuck out of my flat torso like brown
knitting needles. You have to want very hard then, close your eyes
and contemplate them, call one down with the force of your
uncontrollable urge.

If you want badly enough, that is a form of penance. The gods
love the ascetic who buries herself deep in the caves of the forest,
and who lets snakes and ants build their hilly homes around her
bleeding, wasted frame. My urge grew so deep that my eyes sank
in their pits. My hair hung oily and unwashed in lifeless strands. I
grew a squint concentrating on the distant horizon for a sign. When
it came, I saw it at once, and ran towards it without a second
thought.

I had, of course, to respond to my grandmother's years of
over-rich, unadulterated nourishment with a story of my own. It
was impossible to hear her stories year after year, stories of a
womanhood I would soon grow into, without insinuating myself
on to that fantastic canvas.

I lived a secret life of my own: I became a woman warrior, a heroine. I was Devi. I rode a tiger, and cut off evil, magical demons' heads.

With the vision I had acquired through my longing, I saw on the bush beside me a strange, radiant fruit. It was a deep blood-red, and it felt cool, damp with fresh dew. I bit into its thick, succulent flesh, and as I neared the core, I heard a voice say, Are you ready? I nodded my head vigorously, the juice flowing down my chin.

Then I was swept into an eagle-shaped chariot that flew swifter than the wind into the thick, billowing clouds. I choked on the dazzling brilliance of sky and wind. But I got my breath back as the chariot plunged into a dark tunnel among the clouds, and at the end of the tunnel, screeched to a bumpy halt.

Gentle hands helped me out of the chariot. I looked up at my new benefactor. She was a mountainous woman, beautiful, but with the strong limbs of an ox. She led me to her mountain retreat, a humble thatched hut by a perennial spring that murmured in the breeze. She asked me to rest after my long journey. She bathed my feet with fragrant water, and gave me a bowl of clear wine to drink. I felt strong and unweary, totally refreshed.

'You are not beautiful, but your heart beats powerfully in that weak little body,' she said. 'Will you take me for your mentor?'

I bowed low to touch her feet. She raised me up and said, 'Good, we will begin tomorrow. But remember, you must endure pain you have never dreamt of.'

She showed me my bed, a reed mat by the open door. I lay down and looked at the sparkling night below. I listened to the soft murmuring of the spring, and then I slept a deep dreamless sleep.

The next morning she gave me my first weapon, a bow and arrow made of fine string, stretched till it was razor-sharp to the touch.

'Because your weapon is fragile, you must learn to be wily and clever,' the giantess said, and showed me how to shoot the arrows straight and unwavering, so fine that they were invisible till they pierced their target.

I cut my fingers. My back ached from standing ramrod-straight on an empty stomach. Red-hot blisters of blood burnt the skin on my shoulder.

'Concentrate. Think. Plan. Then aim,' she said.

After gruelling months of work, I learnt the magic art of shooting arrows quicker and far more deadly than the blink of an evil eye. Then she brought me a club, an iron chain, a brilliant discus of flames. All these, one by one, I learnt to master.

My pile of weapons grew as the years went by, and my body grew rapidly also, in spite of our meagre hermit's diet; it was now full, hard and relentlessly calloused. I grew three extra layers of skin that kept out the heat, the cold and the evil eye.

When I could shoot a leaping tiger in the eye; when I could swing my club and iron chain to batter an angry boar; when I could throw my fiery discus far, far into the mountains where the wild ones live, then the giantess bathed me as if I were a little girl and dressed me in shining robes of impenetrable armour. She gave me a magic vest covered with little mirrors and told me, 'Now, my faithful disciple, you are ready for your battles with men. Put on the vest only if your other weapons fail you.'

Then I fell at her feet and said goodbye.

'Go, go quickly,' she said, and as she spoke the spring ceased its murmur, and the hut, my home now for so many long, pure, hard years, disappeared.

I met my first enemy the very same day after I had slipped down a long, golden rope that fell down to the earth. I looked around me, at the haystacks, and the fields that were fresh green with rain, and I heard, at a distance, familiar sounds that promised a delightful home-coming.

Then I saw, with my sharp hunter's eye, the approach of an enemy. He was so ungodly, so ignoble, I could have laughed aloud. A fat, greedy man, who kept innocent village girls imprisoned in his harem. He sat on each, one by one, his great stomach crushing them between its thick folds. I met him face to face as he came out of the harem, smirking with satisfaction. One lash with my faithful chain of iron and spear-like spikes, and his head rolled to the ground in front of me, spluttering with bloody agony.

I travelled far and wide, a light womanly youth in my disguise of armour, here marking the devouring body for life, there putting out with one swift arrow the evil eye. After a while, men whispered to each other of the bloody trail that dripped on my path. They called me an incarnation of Durga, walking the earth to purge it of fat-jowled, slimy-tailed greed.

I became famous, a woman more sought after than the loveliest of half-naked, full-breasted nymphs. Men who dared come up to my ear whispered about each other.

'Join us,' some said, 'we will be your loyal warriors, we will anoint you Queen.'

But my heart, crystal-pure as the spring that flowed by the giantess' hut, spurned these fawning offers. I looked far ahead, straight into the mountains, and saw a woodland youth, strong-limbed and supple. I went to him, my shining armour now streaked with the avenger's share of blood. He was young, but wise with his years of seclusion in the mountains, and on seeing my craggy, wind-beaten face, he fell to his knees and called me his goddess.

We lived with each other for ten years and a day. I bore him strong sons and stronger daughters, who jumped to their feet when the cord was cut. My armour laid aside, my body grew womanly and full with a softness, a mellowness that made my far-sighted vision not only keen, but also perceptive.

My husband was a loyal knight. We were perfect companions as we roamed the ravines all day, each shoulder ready for the other's load. At night, as our children slept by the fire, he played on his flute, a bamboo flute that poured out of it high-pitched sweetness, that pierced deep into the dark valley and the caverns of the wild beasts. I sewed two sets of armour for each child, in colours that flared in the liquid moonlight.

When my youngest daughter pleaded with me to go down to the valley with her brothers, I was overcome with the new, yielding trust of my womanhood, and I agreed. She set out like an eager young butterfly, her pink armour glittering like rainbow coloured wings. But she was too young; too untried to survive the dangers of the valley. She came back to us, limping, broken, a rag doll mauled by a careless hand.

My husband took up his hunting spear and his iron rod, but I held him back. I had to pay back the mentor of my youth; appease her with my cupped hands, full of my blood.

I set out again, alone, my breasts held firmly by the old armour, now stretched tightly over my filled-out body. I met my enemy, no fat mass of lazy flesh this time, but an iron-like villain who flexed his muscles and bared his even, sharp teeth as he laughed in wild defiance.

We fought for days on the arid plain below the mountains, each bent on the other's blood. Now an arrow flew past, straight and deadly as a poisoned wing. Now the air was filled with a wild scream of terror, scorn and fury. Now a bloody river flowed between bodies, fresh and sticky with discarded toes and chunks of flesh.

I fought like a lioness that had just escaped long years of captivity. My mane flew behind my head like a banner, and as the angry wind blew through its strands, its roar sounded a shrill pitch, like the sacred conch of a righteous warrior.

I shot my fine arrows of invisible speed; I flung my trusty discus; I heaved the blood-splattered club at his thick, curly head. When I blinked my eyes to clear them of the murmuring dust, he sprouted two sharp horns and a thick, long tail. He charged at me like an angry bull, his tail twirling round and round like a whip.

I hurled a long rope made of a man-eating lioness' tail, a tight noose ready at its tip. It coiled round his chest, but he cut the rope into shreds with quick strokes. We fought on, and as our weapons fell to the ground, he held me in a vicelike grip. We grappled in the dust, our sweat mingling with our grunts and blood. Then he tore off my armour and at the same moment I plucked out his eyes. Blindness increased his fury, and he twisted my neck with his rough hands, his teeth clenched with the effort. I choked, the air filled with the gritty greyness of dust, and I knew the time had come. I laughed aloud, my words slurring with desperate passion. With the meagre strength left in my hands, I seized a well-hidden, trident-shaped knife from my vest. The knife was small, sharp, to the point: a parting present from my mentor, a last resort hidden in a secret pocket of the vest.

As the life choked out of me in big gasping sobs, I aimed for his neck, and cut off his head in one quick, arrow-like movement. Then I lay back, completely exhausted, completely free, and I took one last look at the black sky above, the lone star shining brightly, before I shut my eyes and fell into a deep, smiling sleep.

My mother was not moved by the noble life of the gods. She frowned at my dreamy, inspired eyes which sought something beyond the mundane, literal world she arranged in neat, dust-free pigeon-holes around me. She said to my father, 'This has gone far enough. Your picture-books, her feeble-minded fairy stories of gods and goddesses. I want no more of these fantasies. The girl is almost a woman, she must stop dreaming now.'

The last time I saw my grandmother alive, I had just turned sixteen. I had not wanted to spend my summer holidays in the village. I was not left alone there for a minute; everyone was constantly prying into my new, adolescent secrets. But we had to go because my grandmother was old, ill and lonely for us. Her eyes followed me everywhere as she lay on her bed, a quiet, rasping bundle of broken flesh, not the old friend I loved so well.

To escape her, I spent all morning at our neighbour's house, and crept back warily, hoping she was asleep. Often she was, but sometimes she would call out my name faintly, and I was caught. When we left that year, she wound tightly around the coils of my plait a long string of jasmines. She said it was her blessing, her mother-love that would protect me when my soul was in flight. Two weeks later we got the expected telegram, and she was dead.

After that, everything began to change. I went to a college hostel, and later to America, while Anna and Amma went to Africa for five years. We were never to have a home again. Anna died of his first heart attack, and Amma came back alone to set up this house by the sea in Madras. She was withdrawn, even reticent about Anna's death, and I have had to reconstruct his final hours with the odd details that slipped out by accident.

That distant but gentle face, those large, hairy hands that restrained me with mock firmness, the look in his eyes that betrayed a life beyond my groping demands for love—all these became the stuff of my dreams, images that fuelled wild fantasies every night.

I dreamt often of a god-like hero, a hero who flew effortlessly across the night sky, and who guided me gently when he saw my own desperate desire to fly with him. I also had recurring nightmares, in which the weightless, smooth gliding I now craved was brought to an abrupt halt, mid-flight. He or I, he and I, would come hurtling down, down, and in a chill of fright I would wake up.

PART TWO

1

Two weeks in my new home on Jacaranda Road. Mahesh and I have a large, airy room upstairs with the window-panes brushed softly by the lush jacaranda trees in the garden. The house reeks of character. Nothing here is symmetrical or alike; no concession is made to the merely pretty. A large, wild garden full of old trees surrounds the house, hemmed in only by the tall, ivy-covered wall. The rooms downstairs are like deep, dark, cool caves with their high ceilings, the red and green patterns of mosaic on the floor worn with the tread of generations. The rooms lead aimlessly, one into another, several of them empty. I find it hard to believe that all these rooms were once lived in, that they witnessed the bustle of a big joint family.

Only one room downstairs looks friendly. This is my old father-in-law's haven. The rest of the house is unclaimed, unmanageable, and an old crone, Mayamma, has ruled over these recesses for years. She received me at the doorstep, an unsmiling little figure half-hidden behind my welcoming father-in-law. I am to call him Baba. I have not yet thought of what to call the old woman. I had felt an unforgivable sense of relief when I heard that I did not have a mother-in-law. Now, looking at Mayamma's pinched face, I have my doubts.

It took me at least a week to find my way around the house without wandering into some room or the other, almost apologizing to the rows and rows of ancestors on the walls for violating their privacy. They look strong and grim, prepared for a life of loneliness.

Mahesh and I had a long chat last evening in the terrace garden over tea. He has been a polite stranger in the weeks since our wedding. I can't help admiring his restraint, his detachment which views marriage as a necessity, a milestone like any other. It is a gamble, he says. You measure the odds as best you can, and adapt yourself to the consequences. But this he says in a vulnerable moment of intimacy. Otherwise he does not believe in talking about ifs and buts, at least not with his wife. All that spewing out of feelings is self-indulgent, he says. It is un-Indian.

I find I can barely suppress my increasing longing to say, Yes, we have said enough about your work, your tours, your company. A marriage cannot be forced into suddenly being there, it must grow gradually, like a delicate but promising sapling. What about us? What kind of a life will we make together? It seems too foolish, too intense a question to ask of this reasonable stranger who has already carefully examined, experienced, dissected, and is now ready to file away as settled, something as fragile and newborn as our marriage. Can his acute businessman's eyes, with all their shrewd power, really be weak-sighted? Does he not see that it is too early for quietness? Too soon for the companionship of habit?

A few days before the wedding, I had suddenly panicked. Who was this man, this husband whose arms I was to lie in every night? Horror stories of perversion, blind, bestial lust and impotence frightened me equally. But my waking hours—this was perhaps part of Amma's plan, I would put little past her foresight—were so cluttered with festive details that I scoffed at my own fears.

A month later, watching my husband swing his golf club, eyebrows drawn in concentration, I was amazed by my audacity. Was it trust, foolishness, or a reckless courage that made me agree to this intimacy? I felt I had escaped an axe by a hair's breadth. No, Mahesh is not a pervert, nor is he impotent. As long as the lights are switched off, he is suave, sure, unashamed of his body's needs and desires. And I—not quite innocent but inexpert—am

bewildered by my own response, my acceptance of our nightly
rituals.

When Mahesh left this morning on his monthly tour, I felt like a
child whose summer holiday had slipped away from her when she
was not looking. Tentatively I approached the kitchen, a dark
cavern where witches might brew their potions in comfort.
Mayamma was scraping a coconut. Her long fingers are swollen at
the joints, gnarled like the roots of an ancient tree.

I offered to help, and she cackled a little, then said, 'Here, try
the onions.'

I sat at the large plate of onions on the floor, and began to peel
onion-skin. My eyes and nose filled with the raw fumes as I asked
her my questions about the house, Baba's lunch, questions
expected of a daughter-in-law. She was correct but curt in her
replies, and I could sense her almost palpable anxiety about the
threat of the upstart to her long regime. Slowly, slowly, I must make
her believe that I am not interested in playing mistress. She has the
house, I have, well I have Mahesh.

Baba's room is spacious, with windows all along two walls. He
keeps them open and sits on a rocking chair, chanting to himself.
Baba likes to read out loud. Every morning I hear him reading the
newspaper to himself. Twenty-nine killed in train derailment, he
intones. His years of constant invocation have left his voice in a
permanent singsong mode. I almost expect him to end each
headline with an um or an aha. He is like a precocious old child,
reciting his Sanskrit lessons in a monotonous drone.

I tell him how much I love the house and the garden with its
wild profusion of foliage and weeds. Some old men find it hard to
listen, they are so wrapped up in their monologues about a life
slipping away from them. But Baba is different. He listens
attentively, his hand stroking his white beard. He is an attractive
old man. His aquiline nose, long, narrow eyes, wide forehead with
deep creases, and full lips surrounded by a soft, white bush, give

him the appearance of a dignified patriarch; a gentle pharaoh in retirement.

Baba's father was a wealthy man who owned acres and acres of fields. But Baba knows very little about either property or money. He had himself earned just enough as a Sanskrit professor, but one wall in his room is covered with framed citations and certificates. 'Mahesh speaks of something called management all the time,' he chuckles. 'I'm earning a degree in the management of life.'

When I tell Baba I am interested in music, he shows me his collection of records. He speaks to me of his reverence for the saintly mystics and composers of a bygone era. He feeds me the crumbs of their devotion, of their single-minded fervour.

Baba's stories remind me of my grandmother's, but they are also different. They are less spectacular, they ramble less. Her stories were a prelude to my womanhood, an initiation into its subterranean possibilities. His define the limits. His stories are for a woman who has already reached the goal that will determine the guise her virtue will wear. They make one point in concise terms: that the saints lived according to the laws of time-tested tradition.

His stories are never flabby with ambiguity, or even fantasy; a little magic perhaps, but nothing beyond the strictly functional. They always have for their centre-point an exacting touchstone for a woman, a wife.

Baba switches off the record player and says, 'That is a rare raga, Devi. I named my daughter after it. And do you know what brings this solemn, noble raga to life? It is the *kriti*, a *kriti* which is simple and pure in its deep belief. Listen to how Muthuswamy Dikshitar composed this gem.'

'Muthuswamy Dikshitar had two wives. The first wife was a good woman, but she was as dark as the sky on a moonless night. Dikshitar's parents were worried about the young man's resistance to the lure of worldly pleasures. They found a beautiful, fair-complexioned girl, and presented her to the young *bhakta* who sat in deep meditation.

'Dikshitar accepted her, and his two young wives, like the sun and moon on either side of their unworldly master, accompanied

51

him to Benares.

'Years later, the fair one shyly expressed her desire for jewels to match her beauty. Dikshitar's disciples suggested an audience with the Maharaja of Thanjavur, a patron of the arts who was generous with his gifts of precious gems. Dikshitar looked at his wife, her eyes downcast, her supple womanly body lost in the folds of her coarse, hand-woven sari. He sang, with the slow, regal air of sober righteousness, in the raga lalitha, "*Hiranmayim Lakshmim sada bhajami. . . .*" When I have with me the golden Lakshmi, what do I care for unworthy mortals?

'The same night, the deity, Ambika, resplendent in her glittering jewellery, blessed the fair wife in her dreams. Satiated with the sight of the goddess' divine beauty, the fair one effortlessly forgot her desire for ornaments.'

'Devi,' Baba said, 'wherever you are, remember you are a Brahmin. You may not know it, but underneath that skin flows a fine-veined river of pure blood, the legacy of centuries of learning.

' "A Brahmin," he said, the words of Manu giving his voice a new authority, "shrinks from honours as from poison; humility he covets as if it is nectar. The humble one sleeps happily, wakes up happily, and moves about in this world happily; he who has inflicted the humiliation perishes." '

'I want to learn Sanskrit,' I said.

'Why,' Mahesh asked.

'So I can understand Baba's quotations better,' I said.

'Don't be foolish,' he said. 'The English translations are good enough. And what will you do with all this highbrow knowledge?'

I lay my cheek against the cool, hard wood of the writing-table by the window. The world outside is still, as if in deep mourning. I see Mayamma sitting alone in the garden, rolling puffy clouds of cotton into a strand, a necklace of cotton that will be dabbed here and there with turmeric and placed on the doorstep. Who does it appease, who and what does it ward off? Snakes, demons, mythical monsters—how many stories my grandmother would have woven for me this still, sunny morning.

'Mayamma is not well today,' I said. 'She's been lying on a mat in a dark room all day.'

'So leave her alone,' Mahesh said. 'If you fuss over her today, she'll do it more and more often.'

The garden is a deep sea-green cave. Even the rays of light filtered through the trees are mellow and inviting. I sit alone on the large swing, now barren, its rightful occupants scattered, adult. I love it, its hard, brown wood that has stood the battering of wind and weather. But I cannot swing high, it makes me giddy. Perhaps I will raise a brood of joyous, wild children, who will run pell-mell in this quiet garden, leaving behind everywhere a noisy trail of chaos where their grubby hands and feet have been. Or perhaps they will, like Mahesh, be serious and sensible, well-scrubbed, hair-oiled, miniature adults. They will indulge my fantasies of childhood, but will know better.

'Why is the garden such a mess?' Mahesh asked.

'The gardener's mother died,' I said.

'You mean you fell for that old line?' he said.

'But Mayamma said,' I began.

'Mayamma is getting senile,' he said. 'If you want to get things done, you'd better run the house yourself.'

More than a year has crawled by, only my world whirls in smaller and smaller circles, the centre-point the jacaranda-surrounded ancestral house. I know every shadow in the house, the huge copper vessels engraved by an unknown artist, the rows and rows

Githa Hariharan

of the brass gods of the pantheon my familiar wardens.

'Another tour, so soon?' I asked.

'I'm afraid so, what a bore,' Mahesh said. 'I've got papers piling up on my desk.'

'Why don't you postpone the trip?' I said.

'Why don't I pray to be born a woman in my next birth,' he teased. 'Then I won't have to make a living at all.'

So this is all there is to it. The sacrificial knife, marriage, hung a few inches above my neck for years, and I see now that I had learnt to love, to covet my tormentor. I am still a novice in the more subtle means of torture. I thought the knife would plunge in, slit, tear, rip across my neck, and let the blood gush, the passion of the sacrifice whole, all-encompassing.

Instead the knife draws a drop at a time. The games it plays with me are ignominious. It pricks my chin; and when my hand flies up to soothe the sore spot, it stings my elbow. The heart I have prepared so well for its demands remains untouched, unsought for.

After the early rites of initiation, learnt on old knees; the skills perfected under the eye of a jealous mother; the token rebellion, a concession to youth; this then is marriage, the end of ends, two or three brief encounters a month when bodies stutter together in lazy, inarticulate lust. Two weeks a month when the shadowy stranger who casually strips me of my name, snaps his fingers and demands a smiling handmaiden. And the rest? It is waiting, all over again, for life to begin, or to end and begin again. My education has left me unprepared for the vast, yawning middle chapters of my womanhood.

'Why did you marry me?' I asked.

'Whatever people get married for,' Mahesh said. He peered into the mirror and readjusted the knot of his tie. 'Thank God we

54

Indians are not obsessed with love.'

'The path a woman must walk to reach heaven,' says Baba, 'is a clear, well-lit one. The woman has no independent sacrifice to perform, no vow, no fasting; by serving her husband, she is honoured in the heavens. On the death of her husband, the chaste wife, established in continence, reaches heaven, even if childless, like students who have practised self-control.'

'What have you been doing while I was away?' Mahesh asked.
    'Oh, nothing,' I said.
    'Nothing? How do you do nothing?' he laughed.
    'Baba told me how to reach heaven,' I said, smiling weakly. His laughter faded away.
    'Oh yes, Baba and his Brahmin saints from a glorious past. But let me tell you, Devi, Baba is still to learn how things work in real life.'

In between tours Mahesh tells me I look pale and listless.
    'Why don't you find something to do?' he says as I sit staring vacantly at the trees in full bloom. Laburnum, with topaz grapes clustering among the sunlit leaves, brilliant pink and white acacia, cream and lemon-yellow frangipani, hazy, plum-coloured jacarandas. Only the flame of the forest, the gulmohur tree, has not yet bloomed this year. Its fine and generous sprays of deep green leaves stand mute, unawakened, against a wild profusion of colours.
    'I could look for some kind of a job,' I suggest.
    Mahesh looks doubtful. 'You could try, I suppose,' he pauses, cautious. Mahesh is so even-tempered that he can make me feel guilty with a pause, an inward movement of his lips. His lips are thin and nicotine-stained, his eyes clear and piercing below bushy eyebrows that meet to veil what goes on behind the narrow, unlined forehead. I suspect he trims those outward-growing

eyebrows when he trims his neat, thin moustache. But they growl all the same, with a bored impatience, a touchy superciliousness. His disapproval weaves a cunning cord around my vulnerable neck.

'There is so much for you to do at home. Mayamma is getting old, she needs help. If you need to get out of the house, why not join Tara's painting classes?'

Tara's husband, Ashok, works for Mahesh. We see them often and Mahesh admires Tara's boundless energy, her bubbling, infectious enthusiasm. 'She keeps herself busy but has enough time for her children,' he says. 'I have never seen such well-behaved children before. Lucky Ashok!'

'I suppose I could do that,' I hesitate, but Mahesh has already forgotten my little problems. I have been taken care of; my idle hands have been directed to better use.

Tara's flat is smart and modern. Knick-knacks she has made in craft classes for enterprising housewives are arranged prettily all over the living-room. The curtains, the carpet, her nylon saris—everything matches and exudes an aggressive self-confidence. Her hair is always smartly cut, her fingernails are painted a shiny, blood-red.

She was delighted when I called her about the painting class.

'I am so glad, Devi,' she trilled. She reminds me of a plump bird anxious to hatch more eggs.

'We're just six of us, and the class is very informal. And you do need to get out of the house, even if it is only to socialize with boring housewives.'

She giggled, sure that she is anything but boring.

I was the first one to arrive, and Tara took me on a guided tour of her pretty little nest.

'This is the studio,' she announced dramatically. It was charming, with drawings by her children on the walls, macramé plant hangers with trimmed ivy in little painted pots, and a long, gleaming, polished table in the centre.

'I hope we are going to be good friends. We have known

Mahesh for so long, we really can't believe he is married. You lived in America, didn't you?'

'Yes,' I said, pretending not to notice the pause inviting either the amusing anecdotes or the whispered confidences. I could barely remember those two years, that dream-like adventure which belonged to someone else.

The others came in, and there was quite a bustle of introductions, exclamations and curiosity. The manager's reticent wife. Probably a snob. I felt six pairs of kohl-lined eyes appraise me as we sat down to work.

Tara brought out from a cupboard a stuffed eagle perched on a little stand of cured wood. Touched up with oily paint, sprayed with lacquer-like gloss, the stuffed bird was a hideous mockery of the winged creature that had soared high above the clouds in its untamed youth. Its dry, bulging, yellow eye stared at me ruthlessly.

'Come, ladies, today we have this magnificent specimen for our still-life study,' announced Tara, her hands stroking the stiff, brown-black feathers. I looked away and bent over my sheet of paper. I had no idea where to begin, and already my pencil was slipping out of moist, clammy hands.

'Where did you go on your honeymoon?' my neighbour, a youngish woman in jeans and layers of make-up, asked me.

'The company guest-house in Ooty, where else?' Tara laughed, giving me a confidential wink.

The ceiling fan droned on above us, the eagle-eye stared, and all around me, voices and laughter, eager to impress the unfriendly manager's wife.

By the time I got home I felt limp; my crisp, starched, cotton sari cut my ankles. I looked in the mirror and saw a pale, drooping figure, almost as lifeless as the stuffed bird, a grotesque study in still-life.

That night I dreamt of flying again. I flew swiftly, the globe of green and brown and blue maps whizzing past far below. I flew into a castle and when my feet touched the ramparts, I could fly no more.

I walked into an empty room, and turning to leave, I saw by

the door an old hag, grinning evilly, so evilly, that I remembered her from an older dream. After that, the routine of survival-violence: scratch, bite, stab, twist. The invincible ghost staggered a little. I woke up, then slipped back into the dream mid-air, only to find myself in the clutches of an accomplice, his open robes revealing a cruelly bare, smooth, ivory chest.

When I struggled out of the dream, I quickly slipped out of bed. Pacing the dark terrace garden, the cacti around me thorny shadows, I planned feverishly. I would write letters, I would read the books Baba gave me. I would sweep out my floors every night. I would not let strangers leave their baggage full of jack-in-the-box monsters that jumped up at me, their faces distorted by taunting smiles. I would plan picnics under the acacia and laburnum trees when Mahesh was here. We would sit together and talk, and he would forget the gloomy, brooding face when he heard my full-throated laughter. And what if Mahesh builds his grey, impenetrable walls, his heart mine only on holidays? I have my gentle Baba, his sweet wisdom, his rare but brilliant smiles. Somewhere beneath the dry, cracked earth are the beginnings of a spring, wet and peaceful. I will make a garden for him, I will pull out those stubborn weeds with my bare hands. Or better still, I will grow a garden of weeds, those single-minded, wild, common-blooded weeds that plunge their tenacious roots deep, deep into the helpless soil.

An hour before my father and mother were to take their seven steps round the sacred fire, hand in hand, my grandmother led them to their elders for their blessings. Two trees, one peepal, one neem, stood side by side, their branches and leaves interlocking in wedded bliss.

'In my days,' said my grandmother, 'every newly married couple planted a neem and a peepal, and the sanctity of the marriage-trees would fly like a divine cloud across the skies, to guard the happiness of the couple they were godparents to.'

My parents garlanded the trees my grandparents had planted on their wedding day. They fell at the gnarled, rooty feet of their ancestors.

I have often wondered about those trees, those tender bridal saplings that grew so well side by side. Which, I wonder, was the male, which the female? The peepal is bigger, more masculine in its towering strength, but its forehead and arms are tipped with delicate and tapering, fine-veined leaves. The leaf is often pressed between the pages of books, a memory that distils the leaf of green freshness, to bring out the filigreed intricacies of the veins. Centuries ago, the peepal was associated with the mother goddess; it later changed its sex and became a representation of Vishnu. When holy water is sprinkled around the tree to the accompaniment of prayer, the peepal, through its visionary magic, makes a colourful variety of ill omens vanish: the throbbing of eyes and arms, dreadful dreams, and the imminent encounter with enemies. The neem has a finer spray of small leaves; its profusion of tiny, elegant leaves makes a graceful canopy. But it is realistic and worldly. It sprouts functional twigs that clean between the teeth, its sap is better medicine. Did Anna instinctively hold out his garland of jasmines to the peepal, his feminine counterpart?

I spend hours every afternoon, opening dusty rooms and cockroach-ridden cupboards. The cockroaches, spiders and lizards, taken unawares, dodge behind shelves and duck into holes and crevices. Otherwise most of the cupboards are empty. They are empty except for cobwebs, and a fine layer of black crumbs, like dregs from the past; and the familiar, musty smell of something stale and forgotten.

Then one afternoon, I discovered a cupboard that was not empty. Teakwood, solid, hard, suddenly appeared beneath the sheets of cobwebs. A large trunk-like box bordered with thin strips of carvings. Inside there was a pile of old photographs. I looked through carelessly, their solemn cardboard-faces depressed me. Then I found one of Mahesh and a woman whom I instinctively knew was his mother. Mahesh seems to have changed very little. His child's face stares into the camera, already defined and a little pompous, as if he knew he would carry a great company's image on his shoulders.

Then, as now, his eyes looked straight ahead, as if equipped with a camera that would only produce sharp, mercilessly clear pictures. Only black and white, didactic contrasts, no fuzzy, hesitant, self-doubting greys, pinks, lilacs. The chin then was as undeveloped as it is now; rounded, almost not there. I wonder why he has not grown a beard. Perhaps the company directors prefer their pawns clean-shaven so that they can read and move them more efficiently. In the photo, he wore impeccably starched and ironed shorts held in place with suspenders; a stark, white shirt, the collars stiff as if filled with hard plastic. A model child, perhaps on his first day home for a holiday from boarding-school.

The mother was a young woman, possibly in her mid-twenties. Although like all photos of the time this was a posed studio photo, she somehow looked natural. She wore a necklace, a long chain, bangles, an amulet, and a gold belt around the waist of her silk sari, which was light-coloured with a thick black and gold border. But the jewels melted into the graceful folds of her sari; the *pallav* was draped around one shoulder in a casual manner that suggested no vanity or artifice. Most of all, the mild, soft-featured face shone with a tenderness that negated the studied effect of the formal clothes, the jewellery on exhibition. Her eyes seemed unaware of the camera's unflinching stare. They were long and tapering, mild and vulnerable, as if she were thinking of the child whose shoulders her arms encircled. As if she were trying, with her gentle, persuasive arms, to coax some foolhardy childishness into those starched, knowing, little shoulders.

I looked for more photographs. There were several family portraits, four straight figures, two sitting, two standing, wearing clothes so exotic that they seemed to be in fancy dress. Lalita, my sister-in-law who now lives in America and whom I have not seen, is an elegant and unsmiling teenager behind a seated Baba, who is already a bearded professor turning patriarch. Mahesh on his mother's lap, the mother smiling radiantly, an incongruous figure in the solemn, stiff-backed little group.

But one photograph of my mother-in-law was so different from the rest that I took it to the window and looked at it for a long time. She was older in this, more stern somehow. Was this taken just before she left? Or did the unsmiling reserve, the tense straightness of the thin figure on a high-backed chair, date back to a period of plotting escape?

'When I was a boy, I was always jealous of my friends,' Mahesh said.

'Why,' I asked, stroking the bare arm that held in place the ashtray on his chest.

'Their mothers came to school for the mid-term visit,' he said. My hand lay still, unsure of how far I could go.

'There was one,' he said, 'she was my classmate Arun's mother. She was, what shall I say, not exactly beautiful, but there was something self-assured and energetic about her, like one of those modern mothers in glossy magazines. She was a doctor, a senior practitioner in a big hospital in Bombay, but the things she would bring in her hamper for Arun! Cakes, chutneys; everything home-made. She spoke to us as if we were adults. She had just managed to avert a strike in the hospital, nurses asking for more pay or something. I still remember her—I think I must have been a little in love with her.'

'What was Arun like,' I asked.

'He was an ignorant dolt,' he said.

Mahesh has told me very little about his mother.

'She was a good woman,' he said, as if he were writing an obituary for somebody he had not known at all. Baba, too, spoke to me of her only once.

When Baba turned twenty-one, his mother called him aside and said, 'My son, you are now the head of this household. Your father is no longer here to explain, so I must be both mother and father. You are a man now. A man needs a wife to help him with the business of living. I have three girls in mind, all three from decent families. Hema, Parvati, and Mohana. Do you want to see their photographs?'

'No, no,' said Baba. 'If you think they are healthy and well-trained, why should I doubt your word? But I don't like the names Hema and Mohana. They are too frivolous. They sound like back-chatting, tantrum-throwing, modern girls. You can go see Parvati. There's an old, reliable name! Go see if you like her.'

'See, Devi, 'said Baba,'we knew what filial piety meant. We would never have thought of questioning our parents' wisdom. I saw my wife for the first time on our wedding day. We were blessed with a special kind of trust you don't find any more.'

He was quiet for a few minutes, and his hand stroked his beard a little faster, without the usual regular, hypnotic rhythm.

Perhaps he would have said something more, but I couldn't bring myself to ask.

On an impulse I looked for old Mayamma. She mutters under her breath still, and throws unpredictable tantrums. Some days she lies in a dark room and refuses to eat. But she talks to me, if I seek her out and coax her.

I found her squatting on the stone steps leading to the vegetable garden in the backyard, her hands busy as usual.

'Tell me about these people, Mayamma,' I said.

'Who do you have there? Been cleaning your new house, have you?' She chuckled in that raspy way I had found so unnerving at first. At closer quarters she seems less frightening, a dried-up house lizard too harmless to be repulsive.

'Let me see,' she said, carefully wiping her hands on the corner of her sari. 'What do you think of your husband as a baby?'

I could not say anything to that, so I showed her the photos of my mother-in-law. Mayamma peered closely, as if she were seeing them for the first time.

'Parvatiamma,' she said, as if I had not guessed as much. To make her go on, I said, 'Was she very pretty?'

'Pretty?' Mayamma was scornful. 'She was so beautiful, Devi, that her face shone as if a lamp had been lit under the skin. Oh yes, she was a rare beauty.'

'Mayamma, what happened to her? Why did she go away?'

I thought she had not heard me. She held the photograph close to her wet, rheumy eyes, the only part of her body still not overcome by an arid, cracked dryness. She sucked her breath in before she spoke, as if her false teeth, too large for her mouth, chafed her gums.

'She had to go,' she said simply.

'Had to? Was she sent away?'

'No, no. Everybody loved her, how could we help it? I came to her, homeless, when my son died. My husband, that wretch, God pity him, had disappeared years ago. I came to her with only a torn sari over my weeping flesh. She gave me this home. She gave us all a home.

'But it was not enough for her. After the children went away to boarding-schools, she would spend more and more time in the puja room. She fasted, she did every puja I have ever heard of. And she sang; my God, how she sang those *bhajans*. You should have heard her, Devi—her voice was weak, but how clear, how pure and sweet it was!

'Then one morning, or was it evening, I seem to remember darkness, she came to me with a big bunch of keys. "Maya," she called in that gentle voice of hers—she always called me Maya—"here are the keys."

' "Why, Parvatiamma," I said, " where are you going?"

'She smiled and took my hands in hers. "He is expected back tomorrow, Maya"—she meant her husband.

' "You know how to look after him, and keep him comfortable."

'She hesitated for a minute. "Look after the children. My prayers will be with all of you."

'She walked out of the house, a small bag hanging on her shoulder, leaving me speechless. I felt destitute, I felt my mother had died again.

'The next day I was trembling so much when I heard him at the gate, I almost ran away. What he made of my tears and stammering I don't know. He took the letter she had left for him with me, and locked himself in his room.

'Hours later, when he came out, I still stood trembling at the door. "Go, Mayamma, see to your work," he said, almost as gently as she would have.

63

' "But when will she come back?" I asked like a child.

'His face turned queer and he said, "Never again, Mayamma." How could such a gentle voice say such a cruel thing?

' "She has made her choice. For a woman who leaves her home in search of a god, only death is a home-coming."

'It took me many years to forgive such faithlessness. But, Devi,' she suddenly remembered me, 'he was right. As always.'

Mayamma spoke to me for hours about Parvatiamma. I knew more about her now, I knew she had been loving, gentle, feminine. A woman whose generosity led her outward, away from herself. A woman like my grandmother. But Parvatiamma remained an enigma. My grandmother, broken by old age, a wandering mind, and her unending good works, had never stepped out of her village home. She didn't even come to the temple with us. She would stand every evening in the front porch and squint at the temple down the street, hands meeting in prayer, content with a long-distance blessing.

But Parvatiamma had been more ambitious. She had, like a man in a self-absorbed search for a god, stripped herself of the life allotted to her, the life of a householder. Had she misread Baba's stories? Or had she turned them upside down and taken the contradictions, the philosophical paradoxes, to their logical conclusion?

I kept her photograph in my room. Every morning I woke up to see that face, severe but glowing, look down on me like a guardian angel, a mother unseen. But the day I expected Mahesh back from his tour, I put it away in my cupboard.

'I must look for a job, I have so little to do,' I said. My hands spread before me on the table, palms upward, empty.

'What can you do?' Mahesh asked, like a ruthless interviewer stripping away the inessential. When he says the words, they become true. What *could* I do?

'I saw a post for a research assistant advertised in the paper,' I said.

'You need at least one more degree for that,' he said. 'And what will you do when the baby comes?'

'All men,' droned Baba, 'are enjoined to cherish women, and look after them as their most precious wards. Listen,' he said, and I waited for his voice and face to be elevated, taken back in time to the unambiguous, magisterial days of Manu. ' "Fathers, brothers, husbands and brothers-in-law should honour brides, if they desire welfare. Where women are honoured, there the gods delight; where they are not honoured, there all acts become fruitless."

'Women,' said Baba, 'have always been the instruments of the saint's initiation into *bhakti*.'

'When Jayadeva sang his *Gita Govinda*, wrought out of his meditation on Krishna's all-encompassing love, he wrote on *cudjan* leaves with his sharp fingernail:

smara garala khandanam mama sirasi mandanam
dehi pada pallava mudaram. . . .

' "Oh Radha," he wrote his words into Krishna's sweet mouth, "the poison of love has rushed up to my head. Only your tender, rose-coloured feet on my head will chase the poison down my body."

'When Jayadeva came out of his inspired trance, he read these lines, and shuddered at the sacrilegious thought. He crossed out the lines, and leaving his manuscript with his wife, he went to the backyard for an oil bath.

'Then Krishna came to Padmavati, the wife of Jayadeva, his body smeared with oil, and in her husband's guise, he took the manuscript from her and restored the lines. When Jayadeva saw this miracle, he fell at Padmavati's feet. She had had the fortune of seeing Krishna, a blessing he had been denied. He kept the lines in his song of Govinda, and signed it, the husband of Padmavati.

'A great man can see the spiritual greatness of his wife.

'Purandara Dasa, the saintly composer of Karnataka, was a wealthy tradesman who dealt in precious stones. But as his fortune increased, he became more and more miserly. One day a Brahmin came to Purandara Dasa and asked him for money to conduct his son's *upanayanam*, his formal initiation into Brahminhood. The Dasa kept putting him off. Finally, in disgust, the Brahmin went to Sarasvati Bai, Purandara's wife, with his petition. Without a thought, she removed her nose-ring and gave it to the Brahmin. When the Brahmin went to Purandara's shop to sell the ring, the saint was taken aback when he saw his wife's jewel. He sent a messenger home to bring Sarasvati Bai's nose-ring.

'Sarasvati Bai fell in a faint. When she came to her senses, she walked to her chamber with resolute intent and mixed a poisonous potion in her silver cup. As she took it up to her mouth, the potion disappeared, and she saw instead an exact replica of the old nose-ring. The Dasa was humbled. He gave away his property, and resolved to lead a simple, austere life.

' "Non-violence, truthfulness, honesty, purity, control of the senses—this, in brief, is the dharma of all the four castes."

'You see, it takes the wife's flame of dharma, to light within a man, the divine lamp that is rusting with neglect.

'When Narayana Tirtha, believed to be an incarnation of Jayadeva, was swimming across the stream to visit the house of his father-in-law, a sudden current swept him into deep, turbulent waters. He threw away his sacred thread, plucked a hair off his head, and recited the mantra that would make him a sannyasi.

'But the current began to subside, and Narayana was swept ashore alive. He was in a dilemma. How could a sannyasi go to his father-in-law's house? How could he look on his wife's sweet face again, only to call her sister?

'But he, as in the case of all great men, was blessed with an ideal wife. When she saw her silent husband, she saw through the tempting lie he was turning over in his mind. She saw the luminous halo around his head, now shorn of that one hair that had kept him a householder. She went back to her parents, her forehead proudly marked with the dust from her husband's feet. Spurred by his wife's selfless devotion, Narayana was initiated into sannyasa according to traditional rites.

'A virtuous wife is so devoted to her husband that she dies before him, a *sumangali*, her forehead unwidowed and whole with vermilion, her arms and neck still ornamented with bangles and gold chains.

'Great men earn, through their spiritual power, the fortune of a virtuous wife. The saintly Syama Sastri's wife died five days before he did. Thyagaraja's second wife made even more certain of her passport to virtuous wifehood. The day she was to die, she held a *sumangali* prarthana; twelve married women sat down to a sumptuous feast she had cooked with her own hands. At the end of the feast, Thyagaraja's wife presented each of them with the tokens of their status—six glass bangles, green for fertility, *kumkum*, turmeric, two betel leaves and betel nuts. A little mirror, a comb and a small sandalwood box full of red *kumkum* that was mixed with gold dust. Equipped with the women's blessings, she streaked her forehead and the parting of her hair with a glorious, luminous red; then she laid down gracefully, a whole, fulfilled woman, and died. Thyagaraja looked upon her immobile, tranquil face, and wept, "*Tolijanmamuna jeyu dudugu*, O Rama. . . ." "I have now reaped," he sang, "the bitter harvest of the sins I committed in earlier births." After his wife's death, he appealed to Rama to take him too. Ten months later, he breathed his last, the name of Rama on his dying lips.'

And Baba summed up his illustrative stories with an ambitious conclusion that he believed in deeply, though it was cast in borrowed words. ' "By public confession, repentance, penance, repetition of holy mantras, and by gifts, the sinner is released from sin. That which is hard to get over, hard to get, hard to reach, hard to do, all that can be accomplished by penance: it is difficult to overcome penance." '

I brought Baba a letter this morning. As usual, he sat on his large wooden armchair, surrounded by piles of books. A pale film of dust hung in the air. Sitting there, bent over his book, he looked like some wise old gnome from a child's fairy tale. I thought I would leave the letter and steal away, but he stopped me.

'Come, Devi. Have you seen what I have been reading today?'

I sat on his footstool, happy to be his disciple, to be in his room, where even the air seemed abstract and neutral, devoid of unbridled passion.

Baba opened his letter, giving me the envelope with a foreign stamp to look at. I was a child again, collecting precious crumbs from the fringes of an adult world. Baba's stamp, Parvatiamma's photograph, odds and ends nobody wanted. All these treasures pile high in my cupboard, crowding out the heavy silks and delicate laces of my woman's trousseau.

'It is Lalita's letter,' said Baba. 'She has sent me a ticket to visit her in New York. The baby is due in another month.'

'New York?' I gasped, my feet firmly back on the ground again. 'But for how long, Baba?'

What I wanted to say was No, don't go, what will I do, what will we all do? Who will tell me the stories that hold back this yawning emptiness? She does not need you like I do.

But a wife needs her husband, not her father-in-law. Or her father.

'How long will you be in New York, Baba?' I asked again, my voice quavering as I saw Baba, my guru surrounded by ageing jacarandas in sedate bloom, transported to the screaming neon obscenities of Times Square, the sub-human lumps of degradation wallowing in the Bowery. Would Baba recite *kritis* by Thyagaraja in New York?

I saw surprise in his face, then concern. He took my trembling, moist hand in his dry, large one and smiled. 'But Devi, my daughter, you are the mistress of this house. You have Mahesh to look after, and soon you will have your children too. What can an old man do for you?'

I gaped at him, not daring to say a word of the denial that rushed to my lips.

He looked at me too, for a long moment, and I felt the sharp danger of something unsaid. Then he quickly changed tracks, ascended to a higher plane, before I could say anything sacrilegiously intimate.

'Devi,' he chided, his voice firm and confident now, 'whatever is dependent on others is misery; whatever rests on oneself is happiness; this in brief is the definition of happiness and misery.

'You have learnt music, Devi, but have you understood the

meaning of what you sing? Take this *kriti* of Thyagaraja's for instance. When you came in, I was translating this piece of wisdom for an old friend. Would you like to hear it?'

I nodded dumbly. He was adept at slipping away, retreating between dusty, venerable cardboard covers. I waited for him to begin, to turn the room into a lofty temple.

'Tell me, O mind,' he declaimed, 'where real joy comes from? From the wealth of men or a vision of God? Cream and milk or Rama's nectar-sweet name? A carnal mire or the clear, self-restrained Ganga? Worldly praise or Thyagaraja's song of God?

'You see, even a *bhakta* like Thyagaraja had to struggle with his mind to tug it away from transient pleasures.'

'But what about the end, Baba? Did he achieve his goal? Or did he remain a dissatisfied seeker pushing himself to greater self-discipline?'

'The knower of Brahman obtains Brahman. *Brahmvit Apnoti Param.* To question a saint or a mystic's achievement of an end, my dear, is to go in the wrong direction. It is during their struggle, their quest, that they are closest to the Almighty. *Sada Pasyanti Soorayah.* They see him always. That is the end, if you insist on one!'

Later, as I sat among the cacti in the terrace garden, gazing at the gulmohur trees beginning to bloom, I remembered the *kriti* Baba had quoted. I knew it quite differently, a song in kalyani raga my grandmother had taught me. *Nidhi chala sukhama, Ramuni sannidhi seva sukhama.* . . . Neither she nor I knew Telugu, nor did we have an inkling of Thyagaraja's contrast of the concepts of *nidhi* and *sannidhi.* For us it had merely been a beautiful song, to be sung with feeling. My sense of loss—it seemed to me that Baba would go away forever—became sharper when echoed by the half-forgotten strains of the *kriti.*

Alone, alone in the house with Mayamma and Baba's orphaned books, I read a page he had not read to me. I read about a *kritya*, a ferocious woman who haunts and destroys the house in which

women are insulted. She burns with anger, she spits fire. She sets
the world ablaze like Kali shouting in hunger. Each age has its
kritya. In the age of Kali, I read, each household shelters a *kritya*.

'What have you been doing all day,' Mahesh asked, tracking me
down to Baba's armchair.

'Reading,' I said.

'With the curtains drawn?' He looked at the book that fell from
my hands.

'Baba's books again?' he said, bending down to pick up the
book. 'Devi,' he said patiently, his eyes on the page where I had
been interrupted, 'did your mother need books to tell her how to
be a wife? I have never met a woman more efficient than your
mother.' He put away the book on the shelf with an air of finality,
as if a minor infringement had been detected and checked. He
turned to me, smiling, and held out a hand to pull me up from the
chair, but I saw that the smile did not reach his eyes, which were
cool and distrustful.

I woke with a feeling of acute loneliness, a sharp, dry feeling in my
mouth. Fine tendrils of pain criss-crossed my forehead and I shut
my eyes, willing myself to slip back into the unawareness of night.

'Hello! Not up yet?' Mahesh's voice sounded a little impatient.

Like a languid sleepwalker I got up and went into the
bathroom. The icy water seemed to dull the sharp edge of my pain,
and when I found my way to the dining-room, I felt numb,
immune.

Mahesh looked up from his newspaper and said casually, 'Is
everything organized for tonight?' My mind was blank for a
moment, and he noticed it with mounting irritation.

'Devi, are you unwell?' This was not concern; this was a
reprimand.

Baba is no longer here, but I can still hear that quavering,
hypnotic voice: 'The housewife should always be joyous, adept at
domestic work, neat in her domestic wares, and restrained in

expenses. Controlled in mind, word, and body, she who does not transgress her lord, attains heaven even as her lord does.'

'Was your father like Baba,' Mahesh asked.

'In a way,' I said. 'But he was, maybe he was a little less sure of himself.'

'There should be just about fourteen or fifteen of us,' Mahesh was saying, the muscles on his face taut with self-control. 'Do you need the car to do any shopping?'

'I haven't thought of it yet,' I said nervously, the coolness of water rapidly receding from my temples, the pain rushing full force at me. He did not notice, perhaps he did not want to.

'Mahesh,' I whispered, at the point of nausea. He looked at me coldly this time.

'Devi, I know you think these official parties are a waste of time. But surely you don't think I can manage work at the office as well as at home?'

I hate being called lazy and inefficient, but I hate obtuseness even more. I grieve for Baba, he mocks my grief by talking of parties.

Mahesh took my stricken face as evidence of my repentance.

'I'll see you in the evening,' he said, and added as a kind afterthought, 'Call me if you need to.' I felt my anger, my frustration, throb like drumbeats echoing in my head.

'Tell me about your work,' I said.

'What do you want to know?'

'Everything,' I said.

'Well, let's see. There is a lot of paperwork of course, letters, reports, plans of action and targets. Then we have to know what the market wants. More important, some of us have to tell the market what it wants. I'm putting it in layman's terms, it's not as simple as that, but essentially you have to be in touch. You find out what will sell, keep your ears open. You see what your boys are capable of and give them reasonable targets. The rest is up to you. If you are a good manager, you keep them happy, and get them to deliver the goods.'

By the time Mahesh arrived, just a little ahead of our guests, I was to all appearances a cool, poised hostess, immaculate in red and white silk.

'Your mother has exquisite taste,' Mahesh said, looking at the sari she had sent me.

'Yes, she does,' I agreed, and put away the rustling plastic packet in my cupboard.

All afternoon Mayamma had coaxed me with her consolation, little plans to bring back peace. You will get a chance to wear your new saris. And Baba would be proud if he knew what a good housewife you have become. You know how he values hospitality, especially in a woman. I had to smile at her crude attempts. All the same, I felt abashed somehow. I could hear my mother's voice, melting into Mahesh's, saying, but what is all the fuss about? What would I answer? That Baba had deserted me? That Anna had died alone, far away in sun-scorched Africa, in a haze of pain and dust before I could think of words of forgiveness? That I felt an awesome loneliness, a wave of uselessness begin to engulf me the moment I woke up?

I cooked all afternoon as if my life depended on it. Chop, boil, stir. Like silver eyelids the onion-skin slid on to the board, one by one. The heat and smoke in the dingy old kitchen turned my entire body into a map of little streams. I felt my resentment, my aches and pains, trickle away, leaving me quiet, still, resigned.

There were so many people in the living-room that I felt like some kind of a glamorous vending machine. What will you have to drink? Do try the pakoras.

The women sat separately, huddled bundles in silk, faces set with anxiety to please the husband's boss. They all looked the same to me, but I soon found that there was an unbending line, invisible but self-evident, that divided the women into two camps. The superwomen who had husbands, children and careers of their own, however tenuous, made their own tightly knit circle. The others, the full-time housewives, drifted towards each other, their kinship as inevitable and exclusive as that of the first camp. As the hostess, I could pretend that my rightful place was in between, around, on the edges of, all circles.

I sat down next to Mrs Lal, a young, nervous wife, a recent bride. I could see her straining to meet her husband's eye as she answered my uninspired questions mechanically. I followed her eyes and found Mr Lal, a boisterous young man, an executive with a paunch, laughing hilariously as he refilled his glass. A prim, middle-aged woman across the room broke her silence to address Mrs Lal.

'My husband does not take,' she said with obvious satisfaction.

'Take what,' I was about to enquire, eager to quell this pursed-mouth prude. But Mrs Lal, as if this was the signal she was waiting for, picked up her beaded purse, and rushed out of the room, tears pouring down her face. Mr Lal laughed uproariously at a joke and slapped his thigh in enjoyment. I followed his wife into the garden. She stood staring at the inky, dark outlines of trees and hedges, her back to me.

'That Mrs Lal,' Mahesh said, 'what a country bumpkin! I hope you made her feel at home, Devi. She seemed to need looking after.'

'She was miserable,' I said. 'She hated all of us, she hated every moment of it.'

'Hated? That's a little strong, Devi. Poor Lal, it's not going to be easy for him, helping her to adjust.'

When Mahesh finds that not even his public relations kit of jokes and innuendoes will dry the tears, or draw a smile, he turns away and sleeps. Before he switches off the light by his side of the bed, he yawns widely, deliberately, his pink tongue peeping out like a healthy, juice-filled fang.

'Sleep it off,' he says, 'you know you always feel better in the morning.'

What he means is that he won't be there in the morning to see me drag my heavy feet around my precious dungeon. He has better things to do.

But if he is feeling especially vicious or cheated, he does not yawn. He snaps instead, 'This is what comes of educating a woman. Your grandmother was barely literate. Wasn't she a happier woman than you are? What is it you want?'

'Let's have a baby,' Mahesh said. 'There's no reason to wait. I want you to have my baby,' he said, and after a night of purposeful love-making, he left the next morning on a month-long tour.

He is far too civilized to raise his hand and bring it down on my rebellious body. He snarls instead about women's neuroses and my faulty upbringing. Am I neurotic because I am a lazy woman who does not polish her floors every day? An aimless fool because I swallowed my hard-earned education, bitter and indigestible, when he tied the *thali* round my neck? A teasing bitch because I refuse him my body when his hand reaches out; and dream instead, in the spare room, of bodies tearing away their shadows and melting, like liquid wax burnt by moonlight?

2

I sit on the stone love-seat by the wall, watching the sparrows build their nests. Born householders, they don't drop a single twig, sure of their task. The music wafts in faintly from the house beyond the high wall. First a slow teasing of notes, suggestions of melody. A note is struck, pure, a liquid circle glimmering in its completeness, and held for so long that it permeates the helplessly responsive pores of my skin. A warm glow begins to stretch its caress across my body, and the scales sway their way down a zigzag path, a curve here, a detour there, and a pattern forms itself, flowing sensuously like the life-giving waters of some ancient river.

A raga, whole, complete, the deep, masculine voice soaring high in smooth flight. I could sit here, curl up my full, satiated body, and meet death without a quiver.

I met Gopal a few weeks later when his sister, our neighbour, invited us to hear him sing. I went with eagerness, my appetite whetted by the melody across the garden. He was a flashy man in his forties who drank rum and chewed paan between sublime ragas. He was handsome in a crude sort of way, his thick blue-black beard and moustache bristling on a rugged face. Only his eyes glistened with a swift discerning movement on that rocky, pitted face, sardonic and dismissive, as the neighbours chorused their formal, hyperbolic praise. I felt his eyes caress my body, which was taut with expectation, willing him to sing again.

A gentle rain—I can barely see it—turns the leaf a deeper, vibrant green. When Annapurna came to our house, orphaned, her face streaked with tears and raindrops, Anna took her in, and shut the rain out.

She was a distant cousin of Amma's and had lived all her life in the village, safe and surrounded by its petty gossip and superstitions. Two deaths, one after another, and her small cocoon was shred apart. The villagers scurried to and fro writing yellow postcards to distant relatives. Anna and Amma were appealed to. They wrote back. Annapurna came to us, her face quiet and unsmiling, her shoulders sagging with trepidation.

She enchanted me. She was much older than I was, but once she had shaken off her grief, her orphanhood, she filled our house with unruly laughter. She was not made for long-lasting tears. She cried often enough, sometimes over such silliness, that even I was astonished by her childishness. But the tears dried quickly, even quicker when Anna held her chin up and called her a foolish little kitten.

She would make up for her hour of petulant silence then, whirling round in her flowery skirt and half-sari, her plump, round breasts marking little jumps as she played hopscotch in the backyard. Amma watched us, her lips set in a guarded silence.

Annapurna lived with us for almost a year. When I told her, (inspired by my history textbook) that strangers sealed their new found brotherhood with blood, she was eager to adopt me. 'Let's do it properly,' she said, and we pricked our little fingers with Amma's sewing needle. Smarting with pain and excitement, we stood on the *kolam* by the tulasi plant and joined wounds together.

For almost a week she did not tease me about my fear of climbing trees. She crept up the mango tree, her white feet caressing the trunk with familiarity, and threw sour green mangoes for me to catch. As I looked up at her, her long, winding plait of glistening hair, her skirt billowing wildly, her firm, round body like a ripe mango ready for picking, I whispered to myself in a thrall of passion, my sister Annapurna, my very own sister.

Annapurna helped Amma with the housework and played with me when I got back from school. But it was when Anna came home that she would bubble and spill over with her chatter and giggles. Her hair was combed, her face washed. Her forehead gleaming with a large maroon mark, she would stand at the door like a golden goddess, a goddess who shone with barely suppressed laughter.

But the tinkling peals of merriment, the unrestrained web of passionate intimacy Annapurna wove around Anna and me, were fraught with danger. Amma, wise and jealous, a bitch guarding her own, saw it first. She hovered around, watching. At the first sign of temptation, the initiation of an accomplice, she deftly swept into her palm the fragile, budding sweetness. She crushed it, ruthlessly.

When I came back from school one evening, I met an impenetrable silence where Annapurna used to be. She had left while we were away. Amma was dignified in her triumph, but I could see her pushing down the urge to gloat. That evening, dinner was a familiar old enemy. Anna retreated behind a cold, furious silence. Amma held her own. I sat, bereft, under Annapurna's mango tree every evening for months.

Did he dream of Annapurna as I did, a brief entanglement with soft flesh that lingers and haunts? Did he remember that mango-laden summer when bodies met in blood and sweat? Did he call her name when the pain locked about his chest? Anna, Annapurna, I remember. But even my memories are treacherous. When I dreamt of Annapurna last night, she came down the mango tree and clasped me close to her. The song she murmured in my ear was Gopal's.

'I met five men before I met you,' I said. 'And in America. . . .'

'Look, you don't have to tell me all this,' Mahesh said. 'We decided to get married, and neither of us was a child. Why agonize about what happened before? You should stop looking over your shoulder all the time.'

Gopal strolls into our garden every day, his raw-silk kurta

strangely out of place among the coarse, weed-ridden bushes. His music is his life; he walks a straight and narrow path as purposeful as Mahesh's. But he misses nothing. He knows every muscle on my face, he sees the shadow before it falls across my eyes. We talk, he sings. When he takes my hand and brushes the fingertips with his moist mouth, the lush prison around me dissolves into a green blur. I sleep less and less every night. I ache for that drug, that blissful numbness. Waiting for him, even the trees outside do not stir in their breathless anticipation.

Slowly, slowly, the idea comes to me. This familiar ache I wake up with every morning, I must learn to love. The jacaranda blossoms have begun to waft down, soft, gentle castaways. I stand at my window all morning, the stillness of the old house chokes me. The rain never lets up. It patters gently, incessantly, its mild, monotonous message of reconciliation. Only the gulmohur blossoms fill the air with their noise of ripe colour. Gopal is far away in Delhi, singing to beautiful young women whose eyes narrow with longing. I can see his golden-brown silk, the silver buttons reflecting the dazzled eye of yet another star-struck nymph. The raindrops glisten, like unshed tears at the tips of leaves, fresh and green. All too soon, the leaves, lyrical in their burden, give way. In spite of their life together, it seems, there is a vast distance between gnarled trunk and root, deep and still, and the momentary glitter, woken trembling.

Mahesh does not see the rain. It is so gentle that he does not even need an umbrella to protect himself. He comes and goes, always in a hurry. On the Sunday evenings he is here, he plays cards with a group of young men who roar into the wet garden on their motor-cycles. They talk—I can't hear a word they say—and laugh easily and carelessly. I have never seen their wives or their mothers. Their faces blur into one, all clean-shaven smoothness and asinine laughter. Mahesh smiles at me over his cards when I hover at the door. I can't hold the smile. He looks away, frowns at his cards, intent on victory.

'Teach me how to play rummy,' I said.

'But we play for stakes,' Mahesh said.
'I'll borrow some money from you then,' I said.
'Don't be silly, all the others are men,' he said.

I am alone. I listen to the rain and the gulmohur all day. Dark shadows near the well. Was that a moving shadow, an old man from the past stalking me? Or a ghost, Anna come to claim me from my long vigil so similar to his?

The long afternoon stretches before me like an endless, pointless road. My hands ache with restlessness, my tongue is parched with lack of use. The old woman is garrulous enough if I seek her out, droning half-stories about a past that oppresses me like a life I want to forget.

I wrap up my pride, my sense of foreboding, swallow the dry lump, and go in search of her. She is in Parvatiamma's puja room, polishing the brass gods and muttering to herself. Mayamma draws me into the dark room, lined with aquiline-nosed, slim-waisted, swollen-hipped gods, whenever I seek her out. She dabs them with lime and ash; she streaks their foreheads with a blazing crimson. They loosen her tongue, and she weaves hoarse-voiced fragments of the past.

Mayamma was married when she was twelve. She rubbed her eyes and yawned as she leant back in her father's lap. The hairy, bare-chested priest frowned at the girl-bride and said: 'Flourish, without fierce looks and without harming your husband; be good to animals, amiable to everything else; be the mother of heroes, be devoted to the gods and the bringer of happiness. Large-hearted Indra! Shower on this young bride brave sons and good fortune; give her ten sons; and make her husband the eleventh.'

The ceremonial fire, the smoke and the chanting, lulled Mayamma to sleep. Through smarting, heavy eyes she saw her husband-to-be turn to her for the first time, and address her, his words an echo of the priest's.

'Having taken seven steps with me, be my friend; be my

79

inseparable companion. On the darkest nights, let our common path be lit by our lustrous love. Come, let us walk together, with this guiding lamp between us. Let us unite our minds with the same thoughts and vows. I am the word and you are the melody; I am the melody and you are the word. I am heaven, you are earth. I am the seed, you are the bearer. I am the thought, you are the word. Let me lead you, so that we may bear a son. Come with me, lady of sweet-edged words. Step on this stone; be as firm as this stone. Stand firm on it, and defend it from my enemies.'

When the smoke cleared, she went to live with her husband. He grew a little more crooked every day. He ran away from school and gambled with village-corner riff-raff. His eyes turned sly when they rested on a woman's back, bent over her work.

Mayamma's mother-in-law had examined her closely before the match was made. She had taken the girl aside and cross-questioned her about the jewellery she was wearing. Were they hers or her sister's? She tugged at Mayamma's long, thick plait to make sure it was all real. Unable to check Mayamma's insides herself, she had contented herself with the astrologer's promise that Mayamma would bear her many strong grandsons.

Mayamma's mother-in-law watched her slim waist intently for the first year. The second year she broke into complaint. What kind of a girl is this, she said. She eats as much as anybody else, but is barren. Her horoscope is a lie, she will have to do penance to change its course.

Mayamma welcomed her penance like an old friend. What else would keep the roving eye still? Her husband woke her up every night, his large, hairy thighs rough and heavy on her, pushing, pushing.

She woke up at four in the morning and walked among the blue-tipped shadows to the pond. She prayed, made vows, dipped herself again and again in the pure coldness. She starved every other day, she gave up salt and tamarind. She tied little wicker baskets with crimson strips of cloth on the tree dedicated to Jaganmata. She meditated for hours before a pan of clear water, representative of the golden-complexioned Shashti, giver of children. She fed the snakes her rice and curds, she bathed the all-conquering lingam with sandalwood, milk, and her tears of ardour. To appease the evil conjunction of the planets, she offered tulasi leaves at the family shrine, chanting mantras without stopping for a breath. She invoked every day the goddess' thousand names; five hundred times she prostrated herself at the feet of the ever-fertile mother. Every six months she renewed her vows; every six months she invited six Brahmins to a feast, and sent them away with the richest gifts she could lay her hands on.

A woman without a child, say the sages, goes to hell. Mayamma invoked the power of Pratyangira, the well-proportioned one, to stall this tortuous descent. She went in secret to the priest of Kali, the red-garbed priest who prays only at night. He promised her that a goat would be slaughtered the next moonless night; the flesh of the animal would be dipped in fuming liquor and then burnt. The body of Mayamma's enemy, the body that wished hers to be childless, would swell, putrefy, even as the flesh of the sacrifice swelled in the fire.

Ten long years inched by as she pleaded with the goddess, penance now a habit. The goddess heard her as her pleas got fainter and almost mechanical. Her son was born on an auspicious day, Diwali, filled with lights and firecrackers. Eight years later, her husband, worn into middle age with dissipated excess, disappeared, taking with him all the money in the house.

The mother-in-law shrieked in agony. She took away the wooden idol of the family god to her own room; it had been defiled, she said, by Mayamma's years of unstinting prayer. She bathed it in the five bovine, all-conquering purifiers, milk, curds, ghee, fresh cow urine and cowdung. She summoned astrologers from all the neighbouring towns. Mayamma's horoscope, they said, was without a blemish. Her lucky horoscope would lead him back.

Mayamma never saw him again, but she got him back all right. The son, fed on lavish helpings of tenderness and yearning even before he was born, turned sour early. At fourteen he threatened to beat his mother and sold her last pair of gold bangles. The mother-in-law died, whimpering about the curse Mayamma had brought upon her household. Then she was left alone with her prayers, like a moth buzzing around the flame before the goddess, blind with the years of sacrifice.

The wastrel son kept Mayamma busy. She earned a little; she could cook and clean with the strength of a young woman. No longer fourteen, he did not stop at threats. The night she refused to give him her diamond earrings (her daughter-in-law-to-be's trousseau), he hit her with an iron frying pan. The kitchen swirled around her head and she screamed *Devi*, Mother, hear me. Through the cloud of pain, wet, sticky about her head on the hard floor, she felt his rough hands at her ears, grasping, tearing away.

When he fell ill with a high fever, there was no tenderness left in Mayamma's hands. They were efficient, cool, but they withheld reassurance. For two months she sat by him all night, bathed him, and dried the racked body with a soft old sari. He had never been a son to her as much as he was then, now that she had curbed the flow of her pleas. The fever rose and fell, rose and fell till he was reduced to helpless, delirious moaning. The day he died, Mayamma wept as she had not done for years. She wept for her youth, her husband, the culmination of a life's handiwork: now all these had been snatched from her.

When she cleared out whatever was left in the house—rags, remnants of a past she did not need to begin the flood of remembering—she found the horoscope with all the signs of luck on it, whole and intact. She burnt it along with the body of her son, and left the village by the first bus, next morning.

'From that day, Devi, Parvatiamma was my sister, my mother, my daughter. But they all leave, child, no one stays long enough.'

I looked at the rivers of wrinkles and scars criss-crossing her face. I did not know what to say. What does she care for my sympathy, a drop that evaporates even before it trickles down her hoary face? What can a teardrop, shed too late, do?

'Mayamma was telling me about herself,' I said.

'I feel sorry for her too, but don't take it all too seriously,' Mahesh said. 'Those days are gone, and there's no point listening to all her stories about them. You have far too many half-baked opinions as it is.'

I sat all evening in the dark room of Mayamma's gods. The light of the evening lamp cast a faint golden sheen on the face of the brass goddess. The dignity, the arrogance of the features that passed for serenity, were somehow familiar. Why was Amma not called Devi? Smooth-skinned, small-made Amma. Perfect, somehow compact and self-sufficient like a shell found whole by the seashore. Reticent, unfathomable, like the wild song of the sea trapped in the shell, capable of exercising power over the ear that listens, and learns to love.

Like the brass *devi*, she wears her tokens of beauty with pride. I have always seen on her ears large diamond earrings, glittering, flower-shaped, and on her finger a ruby ring, sensuous and coiled like a snake.

The snake in my garden uncoils its long, slithering body like an accomplished dancer, in slow motion, for two years and a day. Then it raises its hood, swaying from right to left, left to right, and strikes.

I had known it all along. The scene plays itself over and over in the shadow-filled twilight. The telegram, the phonecalls, the house bereft of the *kolam* at the doorstep.

Baba, gentle Baba, always in love with death, his lifelong ambition. His room is already one with the rest of the house. The cool rain no longer sprays its windows. Shut up, airless, its book-lined walls are dust-covered; orphaned. The paint peels and curls on the wall. Neglect. Decay. The body was flown back and it came to Jacaranda Road shrouded, mummified. Even the tears are hushed, appropriate for an old man's passing. Strangers pay inadequate little tributes, they pat Mahesh on his back. He is a tower of strength. He thinks of everything. Legal details, old man's whims, the nuances of rituals.

I am a wooden puppet in his hands. I stand by him, a silent

wife, my wet sari clinging to me like a parasite, my hair streaming wetly down my back.

Mahesh recites after the priest his tribute to a dead father. Let your eye go to the sun, he says, let your life go to the wind. For your merits go to heaven, and then walk the earth again. Or plunge deep into the seas, if you find a home among its waters.

The kitchen is closed for the day and Mayamma stands behind me, her face inscrutable, but her touch gentle when she pours water on my head. The rain purifies anything, even death.

Crows feast in the open air. They devour decaying meat. Baba escaped in deep sleep. The pain grasped Anna's chest like iron-hot pincers and seared his entrails. He struggled furiously, his rasping breath craving for air. Like a lizard that has lost its tail, he writhed convulsively, the open wound gaping. Jerk, gasp, splutter. Then all was still, cold, blue.

You escaped alone, you in innocence, you in the tortured grip of pain, loneliness, and guilt. All that abstract nobility hoisted on a lofty pedestal, yet your wife ran away to seek salvation elsewhere. And yours, the one who stayed, nailed you to the peacock throne in the empty, joyless mansion, an impotent figurehead. Was it all a farce then? This offering I had wrapped with tenderness, with my own fastidious hands, was it for this betrayal?

They have let me down cruelly, these friends I worshipped with the steady eyes, the wide open ears, and the eager, half-empty mind of my childhood. Now I am really a woman: a mother in my receding past, a husband before me. I must follow his self-contained footprints, with clumsy feet that stumble at sharp edges and curves.

I never really had any friends, at least not till I went to college. If I brought anyone home, Amma was always there, a figure in the background, her back straight with disapproval.

Later the inquisition would begin. Is she a good student? Does she get a good rank in class? She wanted the best for me, she always said. What she really wanted to ask, was Are they Brahmins? Are their kitchens spotless? And do they belong to our heirloom-filled, pure-casted aristocracy? Her love was too snobbish to caress freely. The only time I remember her touching me was when I lay half-conscious in a fever and I felt a cool, dry hand lightly stroke my face. Even in my semi-conscious state I knew what was expected of me: I was not to let her know that I had noticed, I was to continue to feign deep sleep. And Anna, that gentle, lovable, bewildered hunk of spinelessness, would look away, withdraw into his secret life, of God knows what cunning and clandestine passions and entanglements. Even when his lips stiffened with fury, he only said, let her be, leave her alone, and held me on his lap, yet another picture-book, pure fantasy, open before me.

The grass was tall, uncut, with jagged ends, and in the cool haze of sunset, the weeds stood ramrod-straight like goosepimples on my tremulous skin.

My grief clings like small hooks to the pores of my skin. They love me passionately. I long for them to swallow me, to be obliterated in their embrace. Or for them to shrivel up and drop dead, leaving me free to breathe again.

The vast, empty rooms of the old house were filled with a silence, a darkness that was abnormally profound. Then, out of an age of silence, an unseen lizard called for help in razor-sharp, dry-throated yelps of pain. A quick rattle of movement behind a framed god, no, a brass lamp; and before I could switch on the light, run for a broom, all was still again.

I wish the morning would come. I have walked the streets all night, almost, my heart laid bare, propped on crutches that promise to ease the burning pupil and stretch over it the eyelid-screen.

Jacaranda gives way to gulmohur. Long before the drip-drop of rain, the mauve fuzziness blooms, moist, light and feathery. It was made for floating, wafting spinelessly in the arms of the brutal winds, a perfect woman who can sleep dreamlessly. It is the gulmohur that is the upstart, the noisy tyrant who usurps the purple numbness with her incessant chatter, resounding sighs, loud heaving sobs and raucous witch-laughter. The tongue of desire leaps from the deep, green-streaked recesses of the petals, the wetness wildly spreading. Conspicuous harlot, mother of all men, she preens her full-blooded, well-defined thickness, soft, swollen, juicy with the thrill of sticky bodies peeling off each other, after blazing crimson for a night and a day.

Mahesh's tours get longer and longer. When he returns, he waits for Mayamma to shuffle out of the room with his bags and he turns to me. Any news, he asks. His eyes quickly appraise my body, all bones and flat stomach. No news, I say.

All through the ages, my dear Devi, Amma wrote, women have sought the deep content that comes with motherhood. When I held you helpless in my protecting arms, when you first smiled at my face bent over yours, when you lisped that precious word Amma, what vistas of joy opened up before me! Mahesh writes that you are tired, depressed. Would you like to take a holiday in Madras? Or we could go somewhere cool and fresh, just you and I, and talk about everything, your plans for the future, as wife and perhaps mother?

Who then is the friend given by the gods? demanded the invisible voice of Yudhishthira.

It is the wife who is that friend and safe refuge, answered Yudhishthira.

What is heavier than the earth?

A mother.

What is higher than heaven?

A father.

86

Perhaps that is what I need. A cradle by my bed, lullabies that will soothe the knotted, discordant raga in my mind, all fragment and illusion. Something real to feel, to hold, to bind me down with firmness of purpose. Something like Mahesh.

'Why do you want a baby,' I asked.

'What kind of a question is that,' Mahesh said.

Watching the rain wet the garden around me, I wonder: will it be long before I dig to recover the treasures of my childhood, buried under the mango tree? The frogs croak in chorus. They mock their lust, even as they call their mates in rain-soaked desperation, their fullness close to bursting.

The little fish swim round and round the pond, shiny little flecks of grey, black and orange. I peer closer and see tiny eyes, intent on survival, darting behind the moss. The mother guppy has had babies. I run to tell Mayamma. Her back bent over a bucket of dripping saris, she snorts, 'You had better rescue them quickly, Devi. The other fish will eat them up soon.'

'But the mother is there, Mayamma. Don't all mothers protect their newborn with their lives?'

'She will eat them too. Maybe she'll eat them before the other fish do,' chuckled Mayamma.

And sure enough, when I looked for those minute pinpoints of arrow-like movement, they were gone. The mother swam around, bland and innocent, a picture of supreme indifference.

When I bled for the first time, my stomach cramped in knots of pain, I went in search of my grandmother.

'Don't tell anyone else,' she whispered to me. 'They'll make you sit alone in the room at the back for three days.'

But I was glad the first time was in the village. My grandmother never said anything direct about bodily functions. She ignored my body, the body vulnerable to sudden changes. She dismissed the discomfort I felt, my shyness in the face of a body that was now a stranger to me, saying, 'It means you are a woman now, my child. It means that you will be a mother.'

Even before I could get used to this new idea, she said, 'But Devi, motherhood is more than the pretty picture you see of a tender woman bent over the baby she is feeding at her breast. A mother has to walk strange and tortuous paths.'

I think I knew what was coming, yet I was unprepared for it.

'Listen,' she said, 'and you will understand.

'When the Bharata king Shantanu rode alone near the Ganga, he met a woman who shimmered with beauty. She was dressed in a robe of transparent, watery, blue silk; she wore a belt of pure gold. Pearls intertwined the streaming locks of her wet hair, which was heady with the fragrance of champa flowers. The king was smitten by Ganga, for that is whom the water-fresh goddess was, and he offered her his heart, wealth and the queen's throne.

'Ganga lowered her eyes with a smile of acceptance.

' "Will you promise not to ask me my name? Will you promise not to stop me from doing what I must do?"

'He did not understand her cryptic conditions, so he hastily said, "Yes, yes, I promise."

'Every year Ganga bore the king a son. But for seven years, she threw the newborn into the swirling, open-armed waters of the Ganga.

' "This is for your own good," she said as she drowned each baby.

('I don't like this story,' I said. 'I don't want to hear it.'

'There's just a little more,' she coaxed. 'It's for your own good, my precious.')

'Shantanu watched, his eyes red with powerless grief. But when she held the eighth child high over the water, a tender smile about her lips, the king cried, "Stop! Enough, do not kill this one too!"

' "Then take him," she said, "take him and be father and mother to him. I shall not free him from life."

'Then she plunged into her river that flowed down from heaven.'

My grandmother fed me this story with her bony fingers, just as she fed me the gooey, medicinal potions she brewed when I was ill. She sprinkled it with powdered jaggery, and pretended it was sweet. I played the game by the rules and pretended to get better immediately.

She did not tell me what she thought of Ganga's story. I didn't ask her either; the storytelling went quicker if I said less. But I know now what she would have said: to be a good mother, to be a mother at all, you have to earn the title, just as you have to renew your wifely vows every day.

A letter from Gopal like a mirror. He sees himself, the artist, scaling dizzy heights with arrogance. Come with me, he says. You must decide for yourself, he says.

'I've been to the doctor,' Mahesh said, his eyes not meeting mine. 'He says I'm—I'm fine. I'll fix an appointment for you to see the gynaecologist.'

Yes, I must decide, take the reins of my life in my own faltering hands. Mahesh has found a doctor, the best of course, who will set right, with sterilized instruments, the rebellious organ, the straying tubes inside me. I will leave the clinic with my parts glued together, whole, mended, an efficient receptacle for motherhood.

Gopal, it is better so. In our foolishness, we see both the brilliance of our fire and our sitting by it, still as water. Together, our animal grunts and groans, and even the subtle smiles, cast rocks in the still water. I dream, every night, of lying calm in the water, cold and detached as marble. It is skin that gets in the way. The bed of the sea is hard and firm, and quenched with the still, silent waters, it does not make outrageous demands.

'I didn't know you drank,' Mahesh said.

'But you've seen me drinking before, you've filled my glass at your parties.'

'That is just to be sociable,' he said. 'I've never seen you drinking alone before.'

I walked into the clinic, a huge building shaded by carefully tended, expensive, hanging plants. My hands felt cold and clammy as I saw the waiting-room: pregnant women of all shapes and sizes leaning back on their chairs, staring vacantly, waiting. The air was charged with conspiracy. The burka-clad woman, the slim one in jeans with plucked eyebrows—all had something in common, the bond of their gently swelling stomachs. I saw a woman across the room, pale, drawn, her hands nervously idle on her lap. Her stomach was flat, she would not meet anyone's eye. She could have been me.

After hours of waiting, a nurse appeared at the door and barked, Nirmala Sudha Radha Devi Kala Uma, hurry up. Six of us, five straining to their feet, shuffling their weight towards the voice. We were shooed into another waiting-room, a small, crowded one, where all the chairs were taken. Bored eyes looked up and sized us up. She's six months gone, she looks anaemic, this one should be ready anytime now.

When was I to see the great doctor, the healer of women? I stood in a corner, flattening myself against the wall to compress myself into the smallest possible space. A baby woke up and cried shrilly. The mother moved the folds of her sari draping the already hilly stomach, and began to feed her lethargically, without even looking down at the baby.

A partially closed curtain made a makeshift cubicle in one corner of the room. Through the several inches below the short curtains I saw a high narrow bed, and wooden steps on the floor by it. Some of us looked away, but we could not shut the voices out. Come on, come on, there are others waiting. Spread your legs apart. A faint sound, a whimper or a whine. Come on, said the relentless junior doctor. You should be ashamed of yourself, a big girl like you getting frightened of nothing. Shall I call Madam or will you spread your legs? Nurse, hold her legs. Silence. The spreader of legs stopped whimpering.

'Have you gone?' asked a brisk voice so close to my face that I jumped. Gone?

'Well, actually, I am not, I mean I want to see the doctor about . . . I am not pregnant,' I stammered, my voice loud with embarrassment. The nurse ignored my outburst, my confession in public.

'Are you Devi?' she asked, looking at me with mock patience, convinced I was a moron.

'Yes,' I whispered.

'Have you gone?' she repeated. Seeing my blank look, she pointed to the toilet at the other end of the room. I squeezed my way to the queue, feeling curious eyes boring holes in my back.

An hour later, I was summoned. No, not yet by Madam, but by her 'senior assistants' who sat near the cubicle. A young woman, obviously pregnant, the *mehendi* still a fresh red on her hands, got up to make room for me. 'No, please, you sit. I don't mind standing.' She smiled and sat, silent. The doctors gave me a sheet with little blue squares all over it. On the top left hand was written, Devi, 29. Enrol in fertility clinic. I felt several pairs of eyes reading over my shoulder and returned the sheet quickly.

'Now you must pay attention, Devi. We will mark the right days for you with dots, so, so. Soon you can mark them yourself, join the dots and make a graph. We'll take a smear now, and give you an injection tomorrow. Then don't do anything for a few days. After that you can have.'

I stood dumb, overwhelmed by this official reference to my sex life. Only a few years ago, I would have burst into laughter. But I seem to have lost, along with many other things, my sense of humour, even my girlish ability to giggle. I am someone else now.

The doctors bristled with impatience. What was I to them but a stupid woman who couldn't even get pregnant, the easiest of accidents? Look at the obedient, dutiful wives around you, they seemed to say. They are born wives, they don't need others to regulate their functions and coax them to grow in the right direction.

Yet another hour later, I saw, or rather heard and felt, Madam for a few seconds. As I lay spreadeagled on the examining table, my feet held in stirrups, a nurse's garlicky breath near my face, a white coat with a silk sari showing underneath moved swiftly toward my legs. Relax now, said a firm, matronly voice and just before I shut my eyes, I saw a rubber-gloved hand poised over me, and then I felt its quick, casual probe. Fine, all right. Get dressed, I'll see you next week.

'You have to get up now,' said the nurse devoted to garlic. 'We have a long waiting-list.' As I gathered together the pleats of my sari with trembling fingers, she asked, almost with kindness, 'Have the assistant doctors explained the fertility course to you? Have you understood what you must do?'

'Let's adopt a child,' I said.

'I don't know,' Mahesh said. 'I'm not sure I would feel the same way about someone else's child. But what does the doctor say? She assured me that these new hormones work wonders.'

It is useful to remember that a husband is a man. So is a father. He trembles if you climb a tree, a foolish, unaided girl. He holds you back from journeys, mistrustful of devils, snakes, young boys' legs, books, anything at all. He ties a fine chain of beaten gold around your outstretched neck, he marks you with his name. He drags your hair by its bristly ends, he strips your breasts of those whorish veils of the goddess, their thousand disguises. He holds his teeth apart in mock kindness and sucks like a hungry serpent coiled around your upright nipple. You can feel the tingling of the sweet venom, racing thick and wet through the insatiable glands of your outraged heart. Do not believe them. Do not believe these strangers and casual tourists who barge in on their battleships and moor a year, perhaps ten, in your boneless watering hole, talking of rest and tranquil nights.

After days of namby-pamby rain, drizzle, drizzle, like a senile old man droning the same ineffective formula of resignation, the clouds burst with shattering thunder. All the little secrets and euphemisms that had seeped into the ground, safely hidden by the moist leaves and mauve blossoms, were swept out of hiding, exposed, with the first genuine deluge of rain.

I find that lying alone, late at night in a house not my own, to shut the doors and windows is not enough. The howling wind outside does not know what it is to be shut out. It seeps in through every crack in the floor, the roof, the walls. Like some grotesquely over-eager mother it wails its way in, and engulfs in its hurricane the dormant mysteries of the house; and what seemed a perfectly respectable house, blank, white-washed and indifferent, suddenly reeks with so much life, it's obscene. Shadows emerge from every corner, stirring restlessly. They unveil and flaunt, bold and brazen, all their stored moments of passion.

'Why are you looking at me like that,' I asked.

'You look so fragile, so feminine,' Mahesh said. 'It's hard to believe that you don't want a child.'

Even as he says the words, I can feel myself diminishing. I become a wispy, insubstantial cloud that can be blown out of sight, that can break apart when touched.

I feel myself getting blurred in Mahesh's eyes. The focus gets softer and softer, till everything dissolves into nothingness, everything but my stubborn, unrelenting womb.

The game is over, just as I was beginning to learn the rules. I will store them, but where? And for what use? The fingers ache to express their forbidden tenderness. They wrap and unwrap, obsessively, using the most delicate of tinsel, a package that is all rough edges.

Is there no other way? 'Devi, Devi,' said Mayamma, when without warning I buried my face in her shoulder and wept.

'There may be, child. What does an old woman know? Pray, pray, Devi. Tell the beads till your fingers are calloused and numb with exhaustion. Sit between five fires in a grove of penance for the sake of your unborn son. Find Shashti's head, a smooth stone the size of a man's head that rests under a sanctified banyan tree. Offer the freshest, most luscious of fruits, flowers and rice to the rocky goddess. Drink the potion blessed by Jaganmata, slit a goat's throat at Kali's shrine. Only the goddess knows what knives of pain twist and turn in a woman's heart.'

I sat day after day in the airless room, the brass and stone pantheon surrounding me. In rhythm with the rain they chanted the secrets of the gods as they danced round and round in a frenzy.

Like Sati you must burn yourself to death, like Sati you must vindicate your husband's honour and manhood.

Like Parvati you must stand neck-deep in cold, turbulent waters, the hungry, predatory fish devouring your feet.

Like Haimavati you must turn that black skin on your sinful body into a golden sheen of light and beauty.

Like Gauri you must reap the bountiful harvest that will be yours if you embrace the lingam on the sacrificial altar.

They danced, their frenzy increasing to a manic pitch, into my dreams night after night. But now Mayamma, Annapurna, my unseen mother-in-law Parvatiamma, the maidservant Gauri, my cousin Uma, the man-turning Amba, and even the barely recognizable, bent frame of my grandmother whizzed past as they whirled around, chanting.

Like Durga you shall be a beautiful, yellow-faced woman with ten arms and ride on a Himalayan lion. Despite your grace, you are born to kill. Take up your weapons then. The discus, the trident, the conch shell, the flaming dart, the bow, quiver and arrow, the iron rod, the thunderbolt, the club. A garland of snakes, and as a charger, the blood-streaked lion with the yawning red mouth.

Ride into the dark night, disguised as a beautiful woman, and devour the demons, thirty to hundred at a mouthful.

When that mask of beauty has served its purpose, tear it away. Let the woman with flowing hair, whose skin glows like a dark blue lotus emerge from your body in complete armour, terrifying,

94

three-eyed, four-armed, holding an untouchable's bell in one hand. Smear your face with coal, smoke, and the ashes of freshly burnt bodies. Like the black mother of earth, smear your tusk with blood and grow claws on your hands. Ornament your naked body with earrings made of little children's bones, a necklace of snakes, another of skulls, another of the heads of your unborn sons, and a skirt made of severed, dripping demons' heads strung together.

Kali, you thirst for war, for heroic feats in battle. In the glaring light of the sun, your eyes are smoke-coloured. In the blackness of night, your eyes are many, your eyes are yellow-gold. In times of peace, you lurk hidden in fearful places. In victory, you roar like a dragon that has licked clean the fires of the three worlds.

In my waking hours I am still no conqueror. My petty fears, and that accursed desire to please which I learnt too well in girlhood, blur the bold strokes, black and white, of revenge. I write elaborate scenarios in my mind for the last act—humiliating Mahesh, saying all the things we have left unsaid. I do something bloody, final, a mark of protest worthy of the heroines I grew up with.

In the other scenarios I am the benevolent goddess, above mortal indignities and cravings. You have trampled on your marital vows, I say like Ganga. For that you will be left alone, without wife or child.

I try endless variations on these themes, but even in my day-dreams they reek of cliché and platitude. No words then, no blood, no scenes. Loneliness is a good teacher, almost as efficient as Mayamma's penance.

I will gather together the fragments which pass for my life, however laughably empty and insignificant, and embark on my first real journey. I would like to do better than sneak out, a common little adulteress. But no, that is a judgement I will leave to Amma, the soft-spoken sphinx who directs useless lives so well. And Anna too, a ghost, pure nostalgia, must be shaken off so that I can learn to be a woman at last. I will soar high on the crest of Gopal's wave of ragas, and what if I fall with a thud, alone, the morning after? I will walk on, seeking a goddess who is not yet made.

PART THREE

1

Sita stood in her garden, watching her old gardener at work.

Alone, the house was precariously close to emptiness. She had felt the restlessness that seized her between projects grow and spread like an insidious germ. Her hands idle, her mind strayed aimlessly, here and there, and halted at doors she had not opened for years.

Then, in the midst of pacing up and down, up and down her impeccable, dust-free room, she had looked out of her window. With a practised eye, she took in the flies buzzing over the open compost heap, the beds of lilies dry and drooping.

Appalled, relieved, she planned feverishly for the next few weeks, and then set the gardener to work.

First the compost heap, exactly three feet wide and three feet in height, was meticulously screened. Then, directed by Sita (who even ate in the garden), a swing and a sandpit were put up, again neatly screened and sheltered, this time by a trellis fence covered with button roses.

A path leading to the patio was laid out—just wide enough for a child's tricycle. The patio itself, furnished with rust-proof wrought-iron chairs and tables painted white, was lined with pots of red and white anthurium, palms and dieffenbachie.

The garden was a large, well-ordered one. The driveway was lined with borders of lilies, interspersed with foot-long intervals of neatly trimmed shrubs. The lawn and the borders of crotons (orange, yellow, brown, green spotted with yellow, twirling and spiral leaves side by side with long, slanting ones) made an effectively simple and neat foil to the huge, solitary laburnum that dominated one side of the lawn. This laburnum, planted years ago by Sita, was now a majestic, full-grown tree that almost eclipsed everything around it with its cone-shaped golden rain.

The best pots, the show-piece begonias, bromiliads and ferns, were on prominent display. Every few weeks, the gardener replaced these with even healthier specimens that had been nursed through infancy in the privacy of the backyard.

Sita was also the proud owner (and trainer) of six bonsai trees. Her own favourite, the bonsai gulmohur, had its fine, tendril-like roots exposed to the air, clinging perilously to a little rock that had been specially bought from an authentic Japanese garden. The tree, at least forty years old, Sita told admiring visitors, sprouted only buds, no flowers. Like a childless woman, it wore its ageless, expressionless detachment; its leaves and buds never fell, they were merely clipped with firm, unhesitating clippers.

To the end of the patio, near the walls, was a small pond, surrounded by lush, yellow marigolds. Sita had the pond emptied and scrubbed once a fortnight. Then, when the fresh water settled into a glassy calm, she poured the jar of fish in herself—exactly eight decorative goldfish, and twelve worker-fish, dull grey, but good for keeping the pond clean.

The wall that enclosed the patio near the pond was thickly covered with ivy. Sita had this pulled out so that a young jasmine creeper could climb more easily, in long, graceful, horizontal sweeps. She examined it closely every evening when she drank her tea on the patio. Left to their own devices, many climbers quickly become a tangled mass of growths, new shoots clinging to, or twining round, older ones; instead of neatly covering the supports provided, and filling their allotted spaces. Sita would start the new shoots off in the right direction, well before the possibility of any rebellion. Then she would check every day to see that it grew almost horizontally: a difficult, painstaking job, since the natural growth of the plant is upward.

The tender, clinging young creeper, so eager to be led in the right direction, so rewarding for a trainer, reminded Sita of Devi. She sprayed it herself; insecticide and fungicide once a week, and hormonal growth-helpers once a month. The results were gratifying: in a year, the wall was covered with long brush strokes of sharp-edged, tiny leaves, the milky, ivory blooms shy and promising.

The garden was what she wanted it to be. Leaning back for a well-deserved pause, seduced by the sweet smells in the air after sunset, Sita found herself slipping, in the unguarded moment that came more and more often, into dangerous quicksands. She found herself unable to resist the luxury of remembering; for the first time in her life she gave in and delved ferociously, obsessively, into the life that had been.

When Sita returned home alone in a taxi, her neighbours on the seafront ran to their windows to watch the tearful home-coming of a widow. Sita emerged from the taxi, a slim, graceful figure, the hair greying a little about the temples, but still beautiful, and impeccably dressed, in a deep blue Kanchipuram silk sari that picked up the glare of the midday sun.

Earlier, at the airport, she had spied the band of mourners waiting to receive her. Her husband's family of course, came with their breast-beating grief and tearful promises of keeping away the loneliness of widowhood. She patted her wind-blown hair into place, drew her gold-worked *pallav* closely about her shoulders and walked toward them. A smile stretched her thin, finely curved lips as she greeted them, and asked after each one's new grandchild, the youngest son's medical seat, the third daughter's marriage prospects.

They found themselves taken in charge; the object of their pity, their overflowing sympathy, stood dry-eyed, smiling and chatting as if this were a dinner party coming to a graceful, inevitable end. Discreetly signalling to her porter, she turned around and said, I expect to be busy for the next few weeks, settling down. The house will need a lot of work, it has been unused for so long. She waved aside their subdued offers of assistance. (Sita was, after all, a wealthy relative.) It would be in bad taste, they knew, to ask about his death at the airport, but since she had practically told them not to come home, what could they do? But before they could ask for fuller details, she was in a taxi, triumphant and relieved, her hand raised for a moment as if to wave at them.

Sita leant back against the seat and shut her eyes, grateful to be alone, her first trial over. The driver, luckily, was one of those sullen young men, not interested in small talk about weather, traffic, or her journey. As the car sped along the sun-soaked beach road that led to her house, Sita sat up straight, refreshed, ready for the task ahead.

The gates were open; she had made sure that her flight into the house, away from prying neighbourly eyes, would be swift. Her letter to the caretaker had laid out clear, simple instructions. Buy one litre of milk, vegetables—half a kg of beans and tomatoes, one kg each of onions and potatoes. Rice, pulses, tamarind, the essential spices. All these would have been bought that same morning, plastic-packeted, and laid out on a freshly wiped counter for her approval.

As Sita greeted the old caretaker Shiva, her eyes darted across the spotless driveway to the garden, the portico, her plants—her pride and joy—all still but welcoming, in quiet anticipation of their mistress' expert touch.

She set to work at once. She did not believe in jet lag or fatigue of any other kind. She inspected all the rooms, upstairs and downstairs. The old man hovered at her elbow, grunting in assent to a long list of clear-cut instructions for spring-cleaning the house. Then she turned around and asked him to repeat the list in correct order.

Four hours later, as the sun began its slow descent into the sea, Sita was still at work. The curtains in the bedrooms would have to be washed and ironed; the gardener would have to re-pot the palms and rubber plants in the bedroom verandas; her own saris, ironed before packing, would have to be re-ironed before they were hung in cupboards lined with dry neem leaves to keep moths and silverfish away. Lists, drawn on page after page of a notepad, lay on the gleaming, polished desk which had been her husband's. Tomorrow she would empty the drawers and ask Shiva to light a bonfire in the backyard, along with the leaves the gardener would rake. She had very little doubt that most of her husband's personal papers would not be worth saving. He used to be a lover of literature (two capital L's, Sita would murmur, her fine nostrils dilating with scorn), and he was one of those anti-social readers who made notes as he read, either on little scraps of paper, or if too lazy for that, on the margins of the book itself.

A week later, Sita had the house exactly as she wanted it. The cook, (good, but inclined to be dirty if she was not carefully supervised), came twice a day to cook hot meals for Sita's lunch and dinner. Sita never ate leftovers. I have eaten enough stale food for a lifetime, she said with asperity about her early years as a bride.

Good housekeeping, good taste, hard work. These were Sita's guiding mottoes as she had taken charge as a young bride, slowly, subtly, so imperceptibly, that nobody suspected what strength lay behind those smooth, child-like features, and the soft whispering voice.

Only Sita knew what relentless self-discipline had gone into the making of a perfect housekeeper, a blameless wife. Before she was married (at the age of twenty, late by her family's standards), she had poured all her energies into her hours of practice on the veena. The best gurus—the best a small town like hers could attract—had taught her all they knew, and Sita was a brilliant pupil, quick, deft-fingered and perseverant. She practised for at least five to six hours every day, and at night she slept with hands stretched out on either side, the callouses on her fingers gently massaged with warm olive oil.

By the time she met her husband-to-be, Mahadevan, and his parents, she was playing not only improvised patterns of notes in perfect time, *kalpanaswara*, but also improvising *alapanas*, sensitive explorations into the characteristic subtleties and nuances of a raga.

101

Her interview with Mahadevan's family was, in fact, a mini-concert. She began with an invocation to Ganesha, followed by a long and leisurely *alapana* in kalyani raga. By the time she played an *ashtapadi* about the sweet poignancy of love, *nindati chandana*, her examiners had forgotten about her dark skin and the severe face that met theirs without a smile; they were overwhelmed by her talent and their good fortune.

But the lyricism of *sahana*, the splendour of bhairavi and todi, the wholeness of a *sampurna* raga like shankarabharanam, did little to help the transition from talented bride to efficient, reliable daughter-in-law.

If there was one lesson Sita had mastered in her years of study, it was this: you did not get results with wishy-washy half-heartedness. Tremble at blisters, callouses or blood, and you can forget about a raga whole and complete, a continuous sequence of notes perfectly strung together.

She put her well-learnt lesson to good use those first years in her new home. The long hours she had earlier sat bent over the veena were now spent in the kitchen; or in her little office, (everyone called it that, at first as a joke), the windowless storeroom where she sat all afternoon under a naked bulb, poring over her account books. She plotted and planned with single-minded devotion, till years later, her schemes bore ripe, fulfilling fruit.

She became an expert at managing things, and even more important, at moulding the most moist and fragile of clay into the most effective shapes. The first tantalizing shape that hovered over her, a teasing, distant goal, was Economy. She mastered that first. Four hundred and fifty rupees, her husband with literary ambitions gave her after each month of pushing files in the railways office. With this, she saved; a cabbage here, a spoon of oil there, and the hoard of small change in an old tea tin grew till it gave way to a little pile of crisp, clean notes, arranged in fives, later tens.

Then it was Ambition. This was a harder raga to master; here she could only be an accompanist to her husband's solo performance. And his was a concert that seemed doomed to ramble, bluster about, and fizzle into a mediocre, amateurish ending. The budding maestro in Sita kept up appearances, and the reticent accompanist eased gently, painlessly, into the role of conductor, the guru behind the imitative disciple's brilliance on-stage. Mahadevan was not a spineless man. He was a dreamer (he liked to think of himself as an idealist), who would suddenly wake up to notice the unexpected detail that had escaped the more alert, common sense-bound people around him.

A few months after they were married, he found Sita in the kitchen at midnight, ravenously eating the chapatis left over from dinner. He realized with shock that she missed rice: all her life, she had eaten three square meals of rice. Marriage had meant that Sita would have to learn to eat dry chapatis, which refused to go down the throat like sticky, wet balls of mashed rice. This was the sort of detail which overwhelmed Mahadevan. A woman who did not complain, a woman who knew how to make sacrifices without fanfare: Sita was such a woman, he thought, and she had earned his unswerving loyalty. What he did not quite grasp, and when he did it was too late, was that a pattern set early in a relationship congeals into a trap. You can't get out of it without causing pain either to yourself or the other person. And Mahadevan, Sita had meanwhile discovered, could not swat a fly without wincing.

But Sita needed all the strength she could muster to face the big trial awaiting her. After that, it was one straight path to a single goal, wifehood. The veena was a singularly jealous lover.

Then one morning, abruptly, without an inkling that the choice that was to change her life lurked so near, Sita gave up her love. She tore the strings off the wooden base, and let the blood dry on her fingers, to remind herself of her chosen path on the first difficult days of abstinence.

When she cut herself off from the clandestine link with the past, a foolish young girl's dreams of genius and fame, she made a neat, surgical cut. She seemed to forget, along with the stringless veena condemned to dumbness, her own mother, father, the gurus of her childhood. She wrote them the occasional duty-dictated letter, but she could never find a time convenient enough to revisit the town where they still lived, or to indulge in a narcissistic voyage to the small, claustrophobic home replete with dated, obsolete memories.

Now all distractions were laid to rest. Sita was at liberty to take her husband by the hand and lead him from promotion to promotion, till he was within the exclusive circle of fast-rising executives who brought home three thousand a month. And this was, she explained to him with infinite patience, only the bottom rung of the ladder he was to climb. Mahadevan would have said something, but he saw the artist's hands, soft and smooth from lack of use. He said less and less, but he dreamt through long, high-level meetings and earned the reputation of a discreet, good listener.

Either it was this reputation—a pleasant change from the opinionated majority—or Sita's gracious parties where even the *pedas* were perfect, tiny and identical, and to which invitations were keenly sought; or perhaps it was just luck, an inexplicable whim of the gods. But Mahadevan (fifteen years, after all, is just a small chunk of a successful life), became a full-fledged sahib, a Brahmin among Brahmins (pure blood and a healthy bank balance), who could list among his achievements a new car, a chauffeur, three full-time servants and a gardener, the best of schools for his daughter, a pension for that senile fabulist, his old storytelling mother in the village, and a large, renovated old house, chosen, said Sita, for its distinctive character.

Devi was born somewhere around the middle rung of Mahadevan's ladder. Sita went into labour without a twitch on her dark face; she remained impassive, a model patient, during a childbirth the doctor claimed was the easiest she had ever seen. The minute the baby was laid in her arms, free of the umbilical cord, Sita refused to let any of the nurses touch her. She had found a new veena to play on, and this time she was not going to give it up so easily.

But bringing up Devi, a longed-for accomplice, proved to be even more difficult than Sita's long hours at musical scales. Devi was a stubbornly secretive little girl. She would run away from the motherly hand, firm and all-knowing, to escape into her father's room. Or she would sneak into the backyard and play with the servants' children. Even worse, she could spend an afternoon talking to herself.

Sita could never quite suppress a feeling of disappointment as she saw Devi grow into an awkward, thin, acne-ridden, stammering adolescent. She herself was thin, but it was a thinness that was spare, taut, uncluttered. She had just enough muscle to stretch a sheer cloak tightly over the sharp, finely etched bones, with no room for excess anywhere. Her beauty lay in the severity with which her cheekbones, and the hollows of her narrow shoulders, jutted out in keen, decisive curves, almost like the well-chosen last word she was accustomed to having. Devi's thin body was different. She was angular, devoid of those essential suggestions of subtle areas only partly visible to the naked eye. Her thin, tall frame stooped a little, and was, Sita shuddered to herself, almost tubercular. In short, Devi, though quiet and apparently manageable, was also bookish and dreamy, and as much of an oddity as her elusive father.

Sita hated all illusion, however tantalizing a form it assumed. She knew what illusion was: she had seized it firmly by its roots and pulled it out of her soul till the enticing stems of the seven-noted scale, came apart, broken and disharmonious in a cluster of pathetic twangs. Even the more staid and constant notes *shadja* and *panchama*, had been pulled away from each other, as good as burnt bridges. Now the goddess she worshipped was no veena-toting Sarasvati, all femininity and ambiguity; her god rode the most practical, the most tangible (and hence most ferocious) of chargers.

Sita could, and did, rule with an iron hand. She thought for all three of them; and when she could do so without offending propriety, she acted for them, swiftly, decisively, and above all, unobtrusively. Her reign did not always run a smooth course; there were little challenges in plenty. Both Devi and Mahadevan had grown into the sly, shifty-eyed accomplices of a mutiny that threatened to erupt through books, daydreams, gods and goddesses, secret corners, the innocent (and therefore more dangerous) sensuality of a stranger like Annapurna.

Sita quelled these phantoms of rebellion with master-strokes: she banished all the gods and goddesses to their rightful place, the

105

little room with a chain of bright-coloured bulbs that lit out all their mystery and seduction. She sent away Annapurna, well-provided, her fascination blunted by her gratitude. Then she swept out dark corners, quiet afternoons, mystical books. One she packed off to Africa on a prestigious overseas assignment, well-equipped with vaccines for yellow fever, cholera and typhoid, and a silver box of blue pills to hold back the terrors of a weak heart. The other—too young for overt managing—was led down a more circuitous route to a suitcase of gleaming certificates, an air ticket and a non-stop plane ride to a continent just distant enough: America.

There she would become a good Brahmin again, in the wholesome rays of a scientific, antiseptic sun that did not hint at dimensions beyond face value. There the darker monsters of the Brahmin world—the gods, the ambiguous myth—would fall back into a less dangerous, better-lit perspective. Devi would learn that she had to use these monsters, not allow them to overwhelm her with lying dreams of blood, paradisiacal palaces and women turning into men.

But Mahadevan was more tired than Sita had thought. He broke apart, a sick old man in his fifties. He had barely had a taste of his prime, his consort enthroned safely, securely beside him, when the wheels stopped turning and his trembling, gasping hand stopped short of the blue pills. He died alone, in great splutters of brain-searing pain. Sita found him in his room, on his chair, his head laid to rest on a pile of papers on his desk. His eyes were closed, his body cold. Even his last struggle with pain he had kept back from her, evasive and stingy to the last. She lifted his head gently and pulled out the papers, notes for an essay on African folklore. She burnt them before they burnt the body, quickly, efficiently, in a modern, sanitized crematorium. She poured both bags of ashes into one jar and booked herself a seat on the first plane to Madras.

Now all her talents, her well-disciplined energy, were at Devi's disposal. Her letters, not too long, not too frequent, flew across the seas like a magnetic charm to bring her daughter back to her.

Sita believed most in the power of her own magic. But like all good magicians, she knew when she needed a few carefully selected accomplices. She made discreet enquiries, collected horoscopes; more important, she conducted a thorough investigation of all the candidates she had short-listed. Horoscopes were all very well, but as far as Sita was concerned, they were useful props. The real decision, the choice, was hers alone.

The stage was set. The props and chorus were ready, awaiting the director's cue. What could Devi, the innocent heroine who strayed unknowingly into Sita's script, do once the drama unfolded to reveal a life, a will of its own?

Sita wisely gave the younger woman enough room to indulge in a few minor and token tantrums. Then, as the priests droned their mesmerizing, singsong mantras, and Mahesh sat waiting, she led her daughter in rich, yellow silks to the fire she had carefully lit, and fanned till it was blazing a fiery golden. Devi had again been packed and dispatched, this time to a more permanent destination.

Sita could now see her life almost as an entirety; certainly it was too late for sudden reverses, or a fresh start outside the parameters she had constructed, or allowed to be constructed, around her.

But Sita also felt the ache of something finished, the unexpected sense of loss that accompanies a mission fulfilled. With her years of training standing by her, serving her well, she forced herself to look ahead. She banned her mind from trading in memories, confessions, judgements, the what-could-have-beens.

She reduced it all, she compressed it, with her usual painstaking meticulousness, into a simple, unfragmented, one-viewed organism. She pruned and re-potted it sensibly, as she did her plants, and she did it in the belief that it would take in the soil, even if it was the soiled ground of a life devoted to being the ideal woman.

In this mood that hovered around resignation, that soared

107

momentarily toward reconciliation, Sita was not prepared for an unexpected betrayal.

The promise made to her, the promise she had made to herself, was not fulfilled. After months of silence, Sita received a terse telegram from Bangalore, not from Devi, but from Mahesh. Devi has run away, he said. Letter follows. All necessary action being taken.

She sat in the patio all day long, brooding over the telegram, especially the phrase, 'necessary action being taken'. Did Mahesh, the candidate she had betted on, know what was necessary?

Sita's anger was not born of ignorance or insensitivity. She had seen in her life the inevitability of cause and effect, the interplay between situation and options. She was familiar with the bold choice made in youth, and with the elliptical nuances of the choice that had to be dealt with, held in control, in the years that came after.

By the time she received the letter, with the lurid details of the betrayal, Sita was in a fury. So this was what she reaped after years of sacrifice, years of iron-like self-control. After all those quarrels with her husband about discipline for a growing child, won through silent, ferocious struggles, and sleepless nights of thorough, between-the-lines planning, the best of possible lives had been offered to her daughter. And what had Devi done in return? She had torn her respectability, her very name, to shreds. And for what prize? A year or two wallowing in the arms of an illusory lover, in a den of riff-raff; then total, abject degradation, the slime and filth of an uprooted woman's decay.

Sita spent her rage, her acrid bitterness, on the over-pruned plants, the sloppy, impertinent cook, the nosy neighbours and the old men dependent on her for their survival. As if in sympathy with Sita's rage, the rain poured for three days and nights. The sea roared as the rain came pouring down, and the angry, open-mouthed, foam-filled waves almost licked the gates of the freshly painted house, now wet and streaked with mud and rain. The driveway was littered with fronds that had been swept off the coconut tree. The beds of lilies which lined the driveway were choked with puddles, the flowers hanging their heads limply after days of being tossed about in the downpour. Even the potted plants in the portico, usually so impeccably trimmed, and sprayed with water, insecticides and hormones, smelt dyspeptic—too much water, too much lushness that threatened to decay. The earthy, spring-fresh smell of the first rains had somehow degenerated: the garden now smelt of overripe, cloying leftovers. The flowers that barely hung on lifeless stalks were the pathetic survivors of an orgy the night before.

But Sita's resilience was a well-grown, hardy cactus, impervious to sudden changes in weather. She waited till the rain let up, and dismissed the cook and chauffeur. She began driving and cooking for herself. She wrote to Mahesh—no scandal please—she pleaded.

Then, after a second round of ruthless spring-cleaning, in a house that reeked of Dettol, Phenyle, polish, incense and cut roses, she sat down, armed for an even more merciless exercise of introspection. Ready for self-examination, she sat before the relic from her past, the broken veena, freshly dusted, and waited for Devi to come back to her.

2

It was still an hour before dawn when Mayamma stirred, groaned, then hit the persistent mosquito against her face. She peered at the barely visible, tiny corpse on the palm of her hand. A long brown streak of blood kept the mosquito firmly stuck to the yellow flesh.

She got up slowly, and fumbled for the box of matches on a shelf built into the wall. She lit the lantern and gathered together her paraphernalia for the early morning rituals. A neem twig, a small brass pot, ground green lentils, the pale brown, borderless sari she had washed and hung to dry the night before. She walked slowly, careful not to drop a thing, to the well in the backyard. An hour later, as the sun, not yet visible, turned the sky a puffy bluish-pink, she stood at the well, drawing one bucket of water after the other. Everything around her was still; only the thick, braided ropes she strained at made the old wheel they encircled creak; the water she drew gurgled in little plops.

Have you seen in how many places they pierced our noses and ears then? Here, look. One, two, three, four. The ruby and pearl nose-ring hung over my upper lip when I was married. He made me take it off, said it made it difficult for him to kiss me.

Mayamma carried one bucket after another into the old, stone-walled bathroom and filled the big, brass drum. Then she took a fine, thin broom and swept the doorway in front of the house. A delicate, white powder trickled through her fingers as she shaped an intricate pattern on the ground. A flower in the middle, surrounded by diamond-shaped enclosures, one around the other. Then curly little waves bordering all the steps.

The morning was fresh-faced after a night of rain. A gentle breeze blew my long, wet hair about my shoulders as I bent to draw the auspicious flower-shaped *kolam* in front of the house. The dewy freshness, the breeze, reminded me of a song my mother used to sing. The melody that rides gently on the breeze, I hummed, tracing swirling, elaborate curves on the edge of each yellow petal. So you've taken to singing in the streets, have you, you shameless hussy, asked a dry voice behind me. The next moment I felt a swift, well-aimed kick on my bent bottom. It was my husband, back after a night of whoring in the rain.

Mayamma put away the box of white powder in the kitchen cupboard and went into the puja room. The *nandadeepa*, the everlasting sacred flame, burnt low, the wick licking the bottom of the brass cup for the last drops of oil. She refilled the lamp with oil and cupped her hands around the flame to give it life again.

Death is an old friend. I have seen Yama's eyes of fire. He twirls his lush moustache with arrogance. They say you can outwit men. You can even outwit Yama if your tongue drips silvery honey, as did Savitri's.

I first met death when I was four, five. The pond in our village was large, and one quiet corner was choked with startlingly violet hyacinths. If you plucked a full hyacinth, whole and fresh, they said you would have a year of uninterrupted luck. If you stepped barefoot and newly bathed on fresh cowdung, your hair would grow long and lustrous. If you heard a lizard call its mate, that was a moment of truth. You could believe anything you heard then. If you left the beehive and the sparrow's nest untouched, the house would be blessed with children. So they said.

I was always greedy for good fortune. Foolish girl. I dived into the water just as the sun set on the bathers going homeward. I found that perfect hyacinth. But as I hung on to it with all my strength, it dragged me down into the muddy, violet swamp.

Later my father saw my hair floating like a bristly water snake above the bed of thick-stalked flowers. Oh that Yama is a clever one, not so easily met!

Mayamma went into the dark kitchen that was like a cave, the dark shadows suggestive of furtive mice and cockroaches. There was a modern kitchen a few rooms away, but it had been fitted out to welcome a bride. Nobody, not even the bride, had thought of using it. Mayamma blew into a pipe, and the high, single-noted whistling puffed at the dormant fire till it grew full and steady. The smoke smarting her teary eyes, she boiled the milk and made herself a glass of strong, sweet coffee. The heady aroma warmed her face and the coffee slipped smoothly down her dry, grateful throat as she held up the glass, careful not to let her lips touch it.

I waited ten years for a son. Years came and went, so did astrologers. I was destined to have a son, they said. To be taken care of in my old age. I scared destiny away with my over-eager pleas, my weekly fasts, my silent and humble apology to an impatient mother-in-law. She tore my new saris and gave me yesterday's rice to eat. What is the use of feeding a barren woman?

Mayamma rinsed the glass and put it away on a shelf. Then she took a large knife and a cane basket and went into the backyard. She had nurtured the small vegetable patch there for years. Nothing much, just a few carrots, aubergines, cabbages and a creeping bitter gourd, but they were small, fresh and delicious. There was too little of any one vegetable to be of use when the house was full of people. But today, after sixty years (or sixty-five?—she was not sure), Mayamma was cooking only for herself. She carefully pulled out four carrots and snipped six bitter gourds that looked like healthy little caterpillars lazing in the sunlight.

I played the harmonium every afternoon one summer. Thirty, forty years ago? The light streamed in through the window, the warm rays seeping strength into my veins as my fingers ran up and down the keyboard.

Mayamma chopped the vegetables slowly, deliberately, her haunch couched on the wooden slab with a carved knife embedded on the front end. Then she bent over the fire and boiled a small pot of rice.

Devi, that child so easily moved to tears, what does she know of penance? They taught us well in the old days. Penance was my grey-haired school teacher. I hung my new sari to dry. The red-gold drew the sun's rays into its soft folds and dazzled the muddy courtyard. Maya, called the voice of my mistress. What are you doing? Where is the rice I told you to cook early today? And the spices?

I ran into the smoky kitchen and gave her the bowl of spices. I'll cook the rice in a minute, Amma, I said meekly.

You have been admiring your fine new sari, have you, continued the mocking voice. What has your beauty done for you, you barren witch?

She pulled up my sari roughly, just as her son did every night, and smeared the burning red, freshly-ground spices into my barrenness. I burned, my thighs clamped together as I felt the devouring fire cling to my entrails.

The next time it was my breast. Cut the right one open, here, take this blade. Take the silver cup with the blood from your breast and bathe the lingam.

113

No, no, Maya. No rice for you today. It's Friday. No rice today, no vegetables tomorrow, no tamarind the day after. Stop thinking of food, daughter-in-law, think of your womb. Think of your empty, rotting womb and pray.

Mayamma picked up a basket again, this time an ornamented, brass one, and walked to the garden. She filled the basket with fresh flowers, wet and sweet-smelling. Red, blue and yellow hibiscus with petals like oily duck feathers; pale, luminous frangipani with lemon-yellow tongues; red-black roses like bits of scented fur; and three types of jasmines, one small and exquisite, the other large-petaled, and the third streaked with radiant orange at the tip of its throat.

She held her breath if a flower brushed past her nose. They would want to smell it first; the scent was for divine noses only. Red roses for Shiva, white jasmine for Vishnu; lotus for Lakshmi, yellow frangipani for Sarasvati; mango blossoms for Kama, red lotuses for the sun, and to placate the doom-loving eye of Saturn, blue, incandescent hibiscus.

The body lay still, inert. The face, freshly wiped with a damp, soft cloth, was no longer menacing. All the rage and fury had been smoothed out, and the face fell back into even, polished, marble features, the innocent, downy softness I had held to my breast long ago. I lit the mud lamp to see better, to keep me company during my last vigil. By the dim, moving light I saw the tattered room, its corners heaped with sheets still wet with urine and vomit. I opened the small window, but even the cool night air could not draw away the sweet, acrid staleness that hung like a thick vapour inside.

Carrying her basket of flowers, Mayamma went into the room of the gods. First she swept the floor clean of a fine layer of dust and yesterday's withered offerings. Then she gingerly moved aside the pictures on the walls to chase away the lizards that hid behind them.

She sat, her feet tucked under her, and began polishing the gods.

The guilt has grown so long in my womb, I find it hard to remember. Was there a time before it began to bleed, ripe for a new life? Blood, O *devi*, I have seen enough blood.

The blood that flowed down my bare leg, hot and sticky, that afternoon when I played in the temple. The hairy priest with a pot-belly called me aside. I looked down at the blood on clear, white flesh, my heart overflowing with something like pride.

Go home, he hissed, and before I could turn around to run, his heavy hand marked my cheek with a stinging slap. Hussy that I was, I had stained the purity of the temple with my gushing womanhood.

One by one Mayamma picked up the gods; and with the familiar hands of a lover, she scrubbed them with lime dipped in ash. They shone a dull, unearthly golden, and she lined them up, each in its place. Then she traced huge, extravagant *kolams* on the floor with a wet, white paste.

My blood flowed freely, I was a woman earlier than all my playmates. I sat alone in the courtyard at the back, three days of the month.

Then the village astrologer, invited with a plate of thick oozing *jilebis*, paid us a visit. The *jilebis* must have been rich and good. He smacked his lips over my horoscope and said, no trouble, no trouble. All the signs of luck are here, she will be welcomed in any house with a son like a young god. Then, when he saw the smiling faces around him, smirking as if the job was already done, he drew his chest out of the soft, flabby paunch and chanted in an oily, syrupy, singsong voice: 'The moon marries a girl when her beauty spreads; the heavenly choir, when her bosom grows; the fire, upon

115

her monthly flow. A maid, therefore, must be wed, before her womanhood develops; no loving parents in fact need wait, beyond the early age of eight.'

My mother made me a feast with her own hands. Two kinds of *payasam*, one with saffron, marked the corners of my plantain leaf. May you always feast in your new home, my little one, Amma whispered. I stroked my new silk sari and smiled impatiently.

The lone housekeeper of the gods now, Mayamma roused herself to perform a full-fledged puja. She lit the numerous brass and silver lamps. She placed little cups of rice and sesame seeds, and a plate of fruit, next to the lamps, on the left side of the gods; the rice thickened with milk and sugar she placed on their right side. She wove garlands of jasmine and roses with banana fibre dipped in water. She lit six sticks of incense and stuck them into a brass stand covered with tiny holes.

Oh, I must have looked like a divine Lakshmi when I went to my husband's house. I was a strong girl, tall and strapping. I stained my soft cheeks with turmeric. I streaked my forehead and the parting of my hair with bloody crimson, and set to work. I put away the shells, the smooth, round pebbles I had played with in my parents' home. I took into my hands the iron skillet and blew the fire into the stove even before my mother-in-law woke up. I cooked for so many hungry mouths. Twenty, thirty? The house was full of brothers, nephews and nieces. I drew water from the well. I scooped handfuls of fresh, wet cowdung and patted the nauseous mess into identical round cakes. With the best of the dung, I swept the floors clean. See, see, the fine grains of filth live on in my fingernails.

I sat at my mother-in-law's feet every night, massaging her fleshy ankles. Close to midnight, she would wake up and say, You can go upstairs now, Maya. You are young, you will want to go to him.

Mayamma gently tossed flowers at the larger gods. Around the smaller ones she hung garlands of jasmine buds. In a broken voice, eerie, hypnotic, she murmured over and over again, Rama, lord of lords, forgive us. Sita, chaste wife of Rama, teach us. Devi, mother goddess, save us. She fell at their feet, her eyes closed reverently.

Devi sat by me, wordless, as I talked to her all afternoon. Once her hand flew up to my cheek as if she wanted it to rest there. Then she pulled it away and it hung limply in the air.

I saw the breast quiver and heave, the strands of hair come loose from the shiny coil at the nape. I knew, I heard the melody that wafted across and made her upper lip glisten with moisture. Somehow, God forgive me, she reminded me of Parvatiamma then.

I knew too, that the day would surely come when she would toss her silks into her boxes, her face streaming with tears, her hands trembling with excitement. I saw her tip-toeing to my room and leaving a small silken bag. She left behind for me, a toothless old woman, an heirloom from her mother, a ruby and pearl nose-ring. The holes on my nostrils are almost blocked with callouses. But my ears, stretched with years of silent listening, sag down to my shoulders; the heavy gold studs I wore on my earlobes for decades have stretched them permanently. Oh silly child, how far will you go with the overflowing bosom and the dreamy, wet eyes?

But I didn't stop her. I couldn't. I heard whispering voices in the rain, one pleading, the other impatient. Then in a voice I had not heard before, soft, mellow, but as decisive as the quick leap off the precipice, she said clearly, I'm coming. Let's go. Quickly.

Mayamma lit a small tablet of camphor on a plate carved with Krishna playing the flute. She circled it before the gods, thrice, with the right hand. Her left hand rang a little bronze bell with the seated bull on its tip firmly covered by her fingers. She put the burning camphor down on the floor, in front of the goddess. She circled her hands round the fire, and held the warmth up to her face. After she had done this three times, she put out the flame gently, careful not to let a drop of her saliva fly into it.

He snorted like an angry bull. He pushed my sari aside even before my head touched the pillow. I was a silly little girl then, his grunting frightened me. If I turned away to sleep, he held my hair tightly with one hand and hit me with the other.

As she kept me downstairs later and later at night, I ran up the staircase to a deafening silence. He would sneak in towards dawn, satiated with his carnal night in the fields, and draw me to himself with rough tenderness.

When I remember, I go into the dark room and lie down on the mat. I turn my face to the wall. Let them cook for themselves. Let them grind the coconuts and spices, I don't eat any of it.

Mayamma swept and dusted the house the rest of the morning. She did not unlock the doors that were shut.

So many rooms shut forever. It is harder to clean the ghost-filled rooms that have no use. Parvatiamma's room that rang with the sound of little cymbals and *bhajans*. The large, book-filled room. He too is gone, the silent, wise one, who was foolish enough to let his wife slip away. Now the child's. She was here for such a short while, but all the corners of her room reek of fresh tears. She haunted the house, day after day, room after room, her pale, drawn face tight and intense. Foolish little one, always asking why, why. Always on the verge of tears, ecstasy. Mayamma, Mayamma, she cried like a trembling little bird against my shoulder. She smelt of sandalwood and fresh rain. Of youth. What can an old woman say? Go? Go for my sake, for Parvatiamma who waited till only Kashi could be her escape?

She ate slowly, her fingers rolling the rice into perfect little balls that slipped into the half-open mouth, her fingers a critical centimetre away from her lips. Then she belched, dryly, without satisfaction, and got up to wash the dishes and put out the kitchen fire. She did not have to cook a second meal today. At night she would drink milk and eat a few bananas. She fastened the latch on the kitchen door so that the stray cat would not slip in.

Five long years after I had become a bride, my cousin came to visit me. He had always been my protector in our childish games in the old village. When I married, he gave me the first gift I have had from a man. A small fan made of sweet-smelling sandalwood, the pieces held together by silken strips of red and gold. Ah, no one in my husband's house knew of those blissful moments of rest I stole, the fan fit for a princess in my hand, laid across my cheek.

He came, tall and god-like, to say goodbye to me before he went to the big city. He had joined the army and was ready to set out on his travels. Look after yourself, Maya, he said, holding his hand out to take mine, then remembering; and his hand limped back to his side, futile.

Write to me if you can, if you need anything, he said, his gruff voice soft and hoarse with tenderness. I put away the fan and the little slip of paper with his address on it in my empty jewellery box. No one will have known, far, far away where his body lay on the battlefield, what noble blood flowed in the body of my childhood friend.

She lay sleepless on her mat, her hands on her sunken stomach, telling her widow's beads. She turned each bead round and round, her gnarled fingers chafing against its dry hardness. She dwelt on one name for each bead, each a name of the mother goddess. Devi, Mahadevi, Sita, Gauri, Uma, Amba. Maya, Mahamaya. Lalita, Ambika, Tara, Parvati, Padmavati, Sarasvati, Annapurna, Lakshmi. The house was so silent that she could hear the occasional knuckle crack as she turned each desiccated, shrivelled bead round and round.

The beads turned round and round. One after the other, deified women with supernatural powers emerged from the

119

goddess' body. Shakti, Mahashakti, Parashakti. Durga, Singhavahini, Mahishasuramardhini. Kali, Mahakali, Bhadrakali. Shashti, Jaganmata, Sati, Haimavati, Pratyangira.

They all spat up blood. The little niece in my new home who throbbed on my lap with a high fever. Earlier, when the diarrhoea began, fifteen to seventeen spurts of slime and blood a day, my mother-in-law glared at the pieces of yellowing cloth I rinsed day and night. What we need, she said, is a purification ceremony.

The next day, as the child lay on my lap, hot and still, my sari soaked in blood and mucus, a hole was dug in the backyard. The old woman threw into it pinches of turmeric, *kumkum* and *vibhuti*. Then fresh lime, uncut, and twelve kinds of hand-picked flowers. Then she summoned the only guardian and doorkeeper she could lay her hands on. A live cockroach, the most stubborn survivor among living creatures, was put into a little matchbox. The mud was heaped over the box, which lay on a soft bed of dew-fresh flowers. The hole—I thought of graves and bent my head before she caught the inauspicious thought—was covered up, and the child, now screaming, was held up by her feet, as if she had just emerged from the womb, her head brushing the newly blessed ground.

The mother knew no ritual to purify the stench of the vomit that flew out of my husband's mouth after three days of toddy and lovemaking in the fields. Then it was her turn. There must have been others in between, I forget. Her blood I cannot forget. Even as the blood gurgled in her throat—blood, phlegm, vomit, she accused me with the hatred in her eyes. I held the pail up to her propped-up head. She brought up all the poison. Her throat began to rattle. She grasped my hand and stared at me, her eyes glazing over with the whiteness of death.

You ill-starred slut, you have brought all this upon my household. Her last words, the blessings of a mother-in-law. She died with her claws firm on my hands, her eyes wide open. I pulled the eyelids down, but they refused to budge.

When Raja was eight years old, I found him the most pious man in our village as a teacher. Raja stood before him, shaven-headed and freshly bathed, his slim legs wrapped in cloth newly-dyed with red chalk, a waist girdle of sacred grass and a strip of deerskin. In his hands he held his father's staff. The guru gave him a cup of water and asked him to look at the sun, all the while repeating the *mantram* the teacher recited. Raja was taught to pray for vitality and strength, to offer fire, to read the *Gayatri Mantram* and to take the vows of a student. He then stood before me, his hands folded in supplication, and begged for his first alms. I showered his hands with heaps of rice and jaggery.

Do what you can for them, but they will twist into the crooked shapes they are destined to fit. Raja I fed at my breast for two years. When he was six days old, I offered six hundred flaming red hibiscus to Shashti, the protector of children. When he was ten days old, I dressed him in a piece of brilliant marigold silk and tied a gold chain of mango-shaped pendants around his shiny, dark, milk-heavy stomach. I painted a black mark on each cheek to ward off the evil eye that might blink at my hard-earned fortune. Then I hid the baby in the folds of my sari as the visitors arrived, and an old woman sang songs to invoke the presence of the gods. In his cradle, garlanded with flowers, and gold chains streaked with sandalwood, lay a plump, smooth stone, gleaming with good health and motherly care. The gods looked, blessed, and perhaps one eye among the hundred darted an evil arrow of envy. The poison wrapped itself like a warm shawl around the stone, and the day was saved. My son lay safe, hidden in my bosom, and I unveiled him then, threw away the contaminated stone that had taken the blow meant for my son. My husband rubbed the baby's tongue with ghee, honey, and a pinch of gold dust. He was now ready for the world, his rightful place in the cradle, just as the gods turned their backs to leave.

Perhaps one turned around for a last look; for a quick parting shot. Raja wrung me dry. The milk would never flow again. Mahesh is no better. He is straight as a ramrod, but you talk to him about Parvatiamma. I don't want her name mentioned in my presence, Mayamma. Irresponsible. Traitor.

Forget her name, forget all those nights she wrapped her

sweet-smelling arms around your sleeping frame. Don't talk to me about the warrior sons in my horoscope, I tell you!

When the goddess blessed my womb and the seed ripened, what joy rushed through my blood! I couldn't walk, I had to skip, run. Talk, sing. Oh, I was mad with excitement and impatience. Even the cursing, which followed me around like a tail, or the raised hand, did not curb me. I floated around breathlessly, awaiting my son. My son to be born after so many years, counted on bleeding fingers.

Now my arch enemy, my mother-in-law, bustled around with purpose, her days filled with the power of her witch's weapons. She ground sharp, needle-like, green chillies and threw the paste into the oil bubbling on the fire. Fire met fire in a sizzling embrace and she smiled in triumph. The form of the evil eye, the vile body that dared to look on my swelling stomach, would now burn, the thick, fresh, stinging paste smeared liberally on its skin. Every time I left the house and came back, she hovered at the doorstep, broom in hand. She muttered to herself and waved the dusty broom before my stomach, once to the left, once to the right. Then she rinsed the broom and hid the dirty water from my radiant eyes. Or for variety, she lit the tip of the broom, and as the dusty sticks crackled, a beatific smile of revenge slipped across her face. The broom got shorter and shorter as the days went by. By the eighth month, it was a charred stump that filled the air with an acrid smell: the remains of what was once a green frond of a flourishing coconut tree.

Then the blood came, too soon, too soon. No expense was spared, my husband wanted the new village doctor, not the midwife. He shoved his greasy hand into my swelling, palpitating womb. I could feel the pull, the excruciating pain of the thrust, his hand, my blood, my dying son. She is strong, she will bear many more children, he said. But after Raja was born two years later, I still groaned with pain.

My womb slips down, sagging with the weight of my greed for motherhood. I can feel it. I need no doctor now. I know it well, its desire to escape. I could put my hand up and pull, pull. Tear it out and throw it on the garbage heap to rot. Raja has no use for it any more. He is reduced to ashes that I fed into the river's mouth. I push it back into place each time, a memorial to my aborted motherhood.

The barber came every month to shave my tormentor's head. Because it was inauspicious to see her at the ritual, stubble-headed, everyone else was sent away. She asked me, every month, to pay the barber and come to her room with a cup of warm coconut oil. My oily hands stroked the smooth little dome till her eyes shut with sleep. I envied her then. I envied her widow's sleep, light and undisturbed.

The evening was hot and still. The rain, incessant over the last few months, seemed to have spent itself out. The gulmohur flowers on the trees were overripe and fell a dozen at a time, squishy and rain-filled. Mayamma sat on the stone steps leading to the house, a paper packet of cotton beside her. As she gazed at the trees and beyond, her hands rolled bits of cotton into wicks. Her hands worked slowly and mechanically, but soon there were enough wicks to light the sacred lamps for at least a week.

Parvatiamma took me to see the moving pictures once. In the darkness I saw a light grow in front of me, divinely bright. Then Rama sprang to life and lifted the great bow. I saw Sita's eyelids tremble on her downcast face. I saw his forehead up close, damp with fine sweat. Then, as cymbals clashed in the heavens, he lifted the bow and bent it. It cracked and fell to the ground with two great resounding thuds. I stood in the darkness, my hands folded in awed humility, and whispering Rama, Rama, I fell at his feet. People poked each other in the ribs and tittered and stared when the divine light vanished and the sunlight came back through the open doors of the hall. But Parvatiamma helped me up to my feet gently. She did not smile. Her face reminded me of a gentle, hummingbird with a broken wing. Her eyes were wet with unshed tears.

Mahesh swore under his breath when I pleaded ignorance, deafness, old age. Of course, of course, he said impatiently, pacing up and down the floors, what do you know of these modern young women? He looked so hurt and bewildered that I put my arm on his bent shoulders. He stopped pacing, and we stood there together, silent. Then he shook off my hand abruptly and I looked up at his face. His mouth was stretched thin and tight with rage. His eyes smouldered with the anger that follows humiliation.

His friends came every evening, and they plotted in low tones against the sound of glasses being filled and refilled. Then they packed his bags, brought him his ticket and he left. For a long holiday, Mayamma, he said. Will you manage the house as always?

The house sat heavily, in a dark silence, riddled with jagged shadows. All the rooms were locked, the big and small windows shuttered. Even the filmy layer of dust that cloaked the empty rooms, despite Mayamma's efforts, lay still, deprived of the faintest breeze. The old house expanded in the darkness; it seized the still moment and stretched, stretched wide to the left, to the right; it grew taller and taller till it seemed to noiselessly open wide its roof, and swallow the world of darkness outside. In a remote corner, like a small, insignificant ant on a majestic mountain, Mayamma crouched on her mat. She sat on her mat, her hands finally idle. She could not think of a single thing to do. She stretched out, bones creaking, and gazed vacantly at the tiles above. Tomorrow, tomorrow, she would plant some fresh new seeds in her garden.

This frail, inconspicuously brown sari, a widow's garment, turns her into a chameleon. In the eyes of the world, she is part of the brown, withering leaf, sunburnt. But what happens if she tears off the shroud that envelops her sagging flesh?

Oh, there was no giggling that morning, even from the village children who were quickly dragged away by mothers with faces averted. My aunt, Lakshmiamma, was then close to seventy. She lived alone in a corner of the dilapidated little family house in the *agraharam*.

Family did I say? Yes, she had a family, and a brazen one too. The rats scampered past her in broad daylight. The mongoose hunted in her backyard. Pigeons rustled their wings in the darkness of the tiles above, and occasionally a swift blue-black wing flew across the room, spraying the air with droppings. She could not see well, but sometimes she felt the slime of a lizard in her rice gruel.

The sole heir to this family wealth, her son, lived forty miles away in a town. He sent her money orders once a month, twenty rupees, and a line to say he was busy, he would visit next year. Then the money orders stopped coming. Lakshmiamma complained in the temple every evening. She wailed in impatient neighbours' homes.

Patience, Lakshmiamma, they said sagely. Money is not that easy to come by these days. Among themselves, they clucked their tongues, and spoke of young men who lost their souls in towns, and old women who lived too long.

Then, for three days, Lakshmiamma was not to be seen. Her front door was shut all day long and the ants quickly built muddy heaps outside the door. The villagers spoke of writing to the son, and clucked their tongues again.

The fourth morning she opened the front door and swept away the ant hills. Then she sat on the front veranda gazing impassively at passers-by. Half an hour later, the entire village was in an uproar.

Lakshmiamma has taken leave of her senses, they said. Oh, this is what happens when a woman lives too long. She casts away her shame, the very source of her womanhood.

Lakshmiamma may have heard the scurrying, and the clucking of tongues. She may have seen the hanging jaw, the wide-eyed gaping stare, and the averted face. But she sat on, unconcerned, stonily silent, stark naked.

An hour later, four old women shooed her inside. They chanted *mantrams*, exorcized the demon, and covered her body.

A few weeks later, the son arrived, looking shifty. Lakshmiamma followed him to the bus stop, meek and silent. But the villagers swore they saw a half-smile of triumph on her face.

And so, my daughters, my tale nears its end. I have teased death, courted him, quarrelled with him. He walks only two steps behind me, eager not to miss a single blow dealt out to my cowering body, as I walk the route that leads to his darkness.

I have learnt how to wait, when to bend my back, when to wipe the rebellious eyes dry. So, with this meagre wealth that has fallen to my lot, I say, go, Devi, search for that forest you crave in your delirious youth. Go deep, deep, into its hollows, and into the wild terrors of its dark stretches. My words wing in a different direction and build a nest for the coming of night. Yours, thirsty, seek the river, miles away, where the dim forest gives way to a clear, transparent flood of light.

3

As the curtain rose, the moon-shaped lights in the hall dimmed softly, graciously making way for a more brilliant star. The musicians picked up their instruments and began tuning them, as if they were indifferent to the encouraging applause of the audience.

Gopal sat centre-stage, his glossy head against the tanpura, eyes closed to help him reach the perfect pitch. Then he handed over the tanpura to one of his pupils, who sat beside him. With one long, slim finger, Gopal elegantly tapped the microphone in front of him. He looked around the hall, at the faces turned toward him, set in anticipation, and the silence amplified his deliberate knocks. Satisfied, he nodded curtly in the direction of the accompanists and their instruments.

Devi sat in the darkness like the rest of them, her eyes on the stage. By now, having been part of Gopal's entourage for months, she knew what to expect. His music was no longer a distant call, romantic because unknown, magnetic because her own experience was so splintered and light-weight.

She felt heavy now, weighed down with the knowledge she had earlier craved so ardently, so youthfully. She had seen, touched, and drawn out, in between ragas, a willing and utterly uninhibited Gopal. She knew the man now, but still did not understand his music. Just as she had known Mahesh's bitterness about the fatherhood that escaped him, but not the source of that atavistic yearning for a descendant.

She felt like an ignorant child imprisoned in a woman's body, displaying, like a badge, her rebellious, independent spirit. But she cowered inside, planning in furtive dread, while another, more defiant self, grasped, filled itself, with odd, exotic and futile knick-knacks of experience. But this bold adventuress soon floundered; and struggled blindly to bring herself to a standstill.

Yet when she heard his music again, the voice against the strings of the tanpura trickling tentatively into the silent concert hall, Devi felt the taut muscles of her neck loosen. She felt a freshness down her spine like the first drizzle at the end of summer. She leaned back and closed her eyes. She no longer needed to look, to see the lights, the garlands of gaudy flowers, the pupils' heads struggling free of their necks in eloquent admiration, or Gopal's face in rapture. Even with her eyes shut, she could see, as if Gopal's music flowed past signposts she had learnt to read, when he would lift his hand imploringly to the heavens, or when he would shrug his shoulders arrogantly at the audience and give the percussionist an earthy, conspiratorial wink.

As the raga swelled, she forgot, she was hypnotized into forgetting, the waking hours of the last few months. She no longer thought of the little pinpricks of embarrassment her position in Gopal's household subjected her to. Even the open leering of his servant boy was temporarily forgotten, and the sly overtures of friendship his pupils made behind Gopal's back.

The music did more; it pushed into some remote region of her mind the image of Gopal, the beautiful despot, his body freshly massaged, bathed and perfumed, holding court every evening, all the favoured courtiers women.

Like a sweet-tongued messenger, a wily peacemaker, the music drowned all effort at resistance. Devi drifted in its mothering arms, with the blank mind of the newborn, the dream of a fresh beginning rekindled.

I am no one, she thought, as she was swept along in the rich current of Gopal's voice, I have no husband or lover, only this blissful anonymity in the darkness, filled with a raga that reaches higher and higher, beyond the earthbound demands of passion.

But at the end of every concert, the voice grew fainter, and Devi thought of a kite that had snapped free of its string. It soars, she thought, beyond the clouds, oblivious of the craning neck below, eager for another glimpse.

The power unleashed by Gopal's voice, the promises his music had made, had lost very little of their earlier potency.

But as the months went by, and Devi went from one concert hall to another, sat in plush seats in different cities, the images his music evoked in her were no longer so uplifting, or even neutral.

She now found herself thinking often of the peacocks she had seen wandering around the park near Gopal's house. Crying for attention, the peacock invariably chose a dry, muddy stretch for its performance, the setting a perfect foil to its spectacular dance.

It stretched out its blue-green neck, and slowly, deliberately, raised its thousand-eyed feathers. The peacock danced, its crowned head still and self-absorbed, its plumage on exhibition. The male danced, ostensibly for the peahen, dowdy and offstage, blending into the background, dull brown against brown. She hardly seemed to notice what must be to her a familiar ritual. But two peacocks nearby responded, as if to a signal, and they froze, then spread their feathers, flaunting them.

Devi looked for the bedraggled, submissive peahen every time she saw herself reflected in the mirror-studded buttons of Gopal's kurta. She fled, as in a nightmare that compels the certitude of choice, from image to image, the array of masks and costumes memories of her various, and discrete, lives.

Between concerts and his own practice sessions, Gopal summoned his pupils for a lesson. His pupils were never very sure when they would have their next lesson. But Gopal was equally cavalier about payment. For months sometimes, he insisted that he did not to want to be paid at all. I have enough, he would silence them haughtily, and if one of the more daring pupils began a thank-you speech, he would be cut short.

'Don't degrade the *devi* we worship. That is all I ask of you.

Sing with your soul. Feel the unique curves and contours of each raga. You are artists, not tape recorders.'

Gopal spent almost an hour every lesson just preparing them to sing. His fastidious ear could bear nothing less than a perfect, harmonious *shruti*.

When they were finally ready, Gopal improvised a brief passage of the raga for the day.

'A raga,' he said to his pupils, 'is like a woman.'

A grin or two broke out on the young faces, but Gopal didn't seem to notice.

'You, Saeed,' he said, nodding his head at the thin, pimply boy who sat closest to him. 'Without the gift of improvisation, you cannot be a singer. Think about what I have said, and sing a five minute *alaap* of the raga.'

Saeed's grin vanished abruptly, and his knobbly Adam's apple raced up and down his long neck. He knew that Gopal's praise and condemnation took equally unpredictable forms. Praise could mean accompanying the master on his next concert tour, or an evening of Scotch and mughlai curries. Disapproval could mean being banished from his presence for a month, or a slap across the cheek for contaminating the purity of the raga. And other than the humiliation of being slapped by the guru, in front of fellow pupils, there was also the possibility that Gopal's ringed fingers would draw blood.

Overcome by a feeling of doom, Saeed began on a light, spring-like note. He shut his eyes, hoping to forget where he was. He sang and sang, for five whole minutes, but found he could not get out of a repetitious maze of coy and flirtatious phrases. He ended on a note of uncertainty, vainly hoping that Gopal's experience of women coincided, at some point, with his own somewhat limited knowledge of them. It seemed to him that what made women women was their unpredictability. Their charming fickleness.

The pupils sat in a hushed silence, holding their breath, not moving a muscle as they waited for Gopal to pass judgement. Gopal sat before them, his chin heavy on the palms of his hands, the fingers covering his face.

A few minutes later, minutes which seemed abnormally long to his pupils, he lifted his head and uncovered his face. He looked around at them, his face puffy with rage. He pointed a bejewelled finger at each of them in turn.

'You fools,' he said, 'has any one of you known a woman?'

If he had asked them this question at one of his drinking parties, they would not perhaps have been so tongue-tied. But as it was, all of them, and Saeed most of all, looked totally blank, as if they had been asked if they had ever visited the moon.

Gopal turned to Saeed, who bowed his head like a convict awaiting his sentence.

'You are confusing a woman with your two-paisa tease,' he said. 'Forget your cheap films and your neighbour's daughter who peeps at you coyly through her window curtains. I am talking about a full-blooded woman, a real one with passion.'

And to prove that words were inadequate to describe such a creature, such an inspiring muse, Gopal began to sing.

He began with four phrases that he sang over and over again like a curtain-raiser. Then the phrases broke up, and the notes rearranged themselves into a more complex pattern that surged, thrust forward, undeterred by the minor motifs that continued to recur in the background. The light-weight, more mundane sub-plots, fell into place as Gopal drew out of them one melody, strong and whole, that transformed, with its rich-throated passion, lyricism into grandeur.

He gave himself only five minutes to do this, exactly what he had given Saeed.

'You see,' he concluded the lesson for the day, 'why this raga is like a woman? It is a raga that celebrates strength. It is passion that gives direction to all the superficial, pretty little phrases. You arrange them like props, so that the real heroine can emerge.'

A restless Devi went into the October night with Gopal's entourage. They were driven in a long, white car that sped swiftly across the deserted, tree-lined avenues of imperial Delhi. Gopal's silk-covered thighs pressed against her legs. The hollow base of the tanpura lay hard and unyielding on her lap. A sweet, cloying smell of perfume hung in the air.

In the big, white mansion, surrounded by a large, well-kept garden, Devi felt like a foreigner. The house belonged to an industrialist whose family had been, for several generations, patrons of the arts.

As they entered the living-room, which seemed vast because the furniture had been moved out, a uniformed bearer delicately indicated their slippers. They removed them, as if they were entering a temple, and Devi felt her feet sink into the soft, luxurious carpet that covered the floor from wall to wall.

She sat on the carpet, too self-conscious to lean against the white bolsters on the floor which demanded a position of abandon. A waiter handed Devi a pink sherbet in an icy glass. It was cool, but it had a strange, bitter-sweet aftertaste.

'Friends,' said the industrialist's son, a young man being groomed to take over the business empire, 'we are honoured to have with us today a truly great artist.' And he indicated with a respectful nod, Gopal, who had taken his place among the musicians. The accompanists surrounding Gopal waited; their waiting seemed to have an air of resignation about it. They sat, their hands on their laps, their instruments in their boxes, but not yet tuned.

'Pandit Gopal Sharma was born into a family of musicians in Lucknow. His father took him on as a pupil at the age of five, and for ten years he underwent rigorous training in the basic principles of Hindustani music. He gave his first public performance at the tender age of fifteen, and the renowned Ustad Sajjid Khan, who was in the audience, was so impressed with the boy's talent, and his mastery of *shruti*, that he offered to teach him. The young musician moved to his new guru's house, and, as disciples did in those days, looked after his needs like a loyal servant. The daily hours of practice—his *riyaz*—were as long as six hours at a time.'

His voice droned on and on as he read from a sheaf of papers, and Devi stole a look at the musicians who sat blank-faced around Gopal. If they were not listening, if they did not understand English, they seemed to know all the same, they seemed to sense through their years of experience, when the speechmaking and flowery tributes would end. When the host had finished describing the plans of the chamber music society sponsored by his industrial house, he looked up from his papers, and after an uncertain pause, he cleared his throat and said, 'Friends, I don't want to stand between you and the artist any longer . . . .' And as if they took him at his word, the musicians picked up their instruments and began to tune them.

A little flutter rustled among the spectators as a young woman, in a bright silk sari and a brief choli that showed an incredible expanse of midriff, made her way to the musicians with a garland in her hand.

Devi watched as she swayed gracefully up to Gopal, as if it were her *swayamvara*. She smiled at him, in a dazzle of silk, gold and dimples, and Gopal bent his head to receive her garland.

In the small gathering, an audience the announcer had described as intimate, Devi missed the dark anonymity of the concert hall. With the lights on, she could not listen to the music as if she did not know Gopal. She could feel the appraisal of a straying eye, cool and dismissive, on her face. She knew she was being labelled, and she also knew that if she got up, accosted them and denied the label, she would not convince them. Perhaps they would be a little surprised that she had a will of her own to assert. But the raised eyebrow would, she thought, give way to an amused indulgence, as if she were a confused child throwing a minor tantrum.

'Stare back at them,' Gopal would say if she told him. 'Don't tremble like that. You have those big, angry eyes, why don't you use them?' Then, more gently, he would raise her hand to his lips. He was a most attentive lover when he played teacher. 'Are you ashamed of your passion?' he would ask, genuinely incredulous. 'Of me? Of yourself because you are my inspiration?'

Late at night, the concert came to an end and the instruments were put away. The sherbet-bearing waiters now wheeled in a large mahogany trolley, piled with bottles and glasses. Gopal, a glass of rum in his hand, was surrounded by a thick ring of admirers.

'Panditji,' gushed a middle-aged woman whose hair was orange-brown with henna, 'your singing reduces me to helplessness.' Devi looked more closely at this woman who summed up so precisely what she herself felt. Staring at the woman, now a caricature of ecstasy, her thin, plucked eyebrows contorting with feeling, her ample breasts thrusting forward aggressively, Devi felt a hysterical giggle bubble up her throat.

'You must come and eat in my house,' Devi heard her say. 'And bring your troupe of course.'

'Kalyaniji, we will all come. What would we poor artists do without you to look after us?'

Gopal turned around and looked at Devi, his mouth twisting into a sardonic grin. But Devi knew he would go. Just as he would, after a few more rums, forget his carefully cultivated arrogance and his talk of artists, and seek out the budding patron of the arts, the young industrialist.

The evening did not end when they left the mansion. Their back-slapping camaraderie was only the prelude to the revels of a less inhibited, more boisterous crowd that gravitated toward Gopal's house.

'Have a drink, Devi,' said Gopal, his rum and paan breath an inch from her face, 'let's celebrate. If everything goes well, your panditji will be in America next month. Eight cities in three months, all expenses paid.'

So Gopal had played his cards well, Devi thought, he has sung for the right people tonight.

'Will you come with me?' he whispered, his voice slipping down to an amorous pitch. But before Devi could answer him, a man with his silk kurta unbuttoned to reveal a flabby, hairy chest, put his arm around Gopal's shoulders and pulled him away.

'Look at him, Deviji,' he pouted coyly. 'You have the rest of the night, and already he is trying to run away from his friends.' The pout turned into a leer, and he flashed his paan-stained teeth at Devi.

She sat alone, watching. The whisky she had drunk rolled around her empty stomach like a dry, fiery ball. She looked around her, eyes sharpened by the unforgiving burning inside.

She saw the props of a performer. The fawning yes-men, the giggling pupils unsure of the master's next whim, the stray women absorbed in a familiar game. The room filled with the sharp, pungent smell of smoke and stale perfume. She heard, somewhere between the laughter and drink-induced confessions, a male voice quoting Urdu couplets.

'My heart is a slave,' he declaimed, his voice tearful with rum, 'and my mind is a tyrannical master. Only you can stem this flow of blood; only you can break the walls that imprison me.' The woman whose arm he lunged towards pushed him away, laughing. A glass broke somewhere in the room.

In her isolated corner, an outsider forever on the fringes of a less ambivalent identity, Devi remembered her last day in America. With a piercing clarity, as if she had dreamt the years in between, she saw the pale, ghost-like figure of Fellini's Casanova. But what she saw now, in undeniable flesh and blood before her, was no bogeyman in a young girl's dreams. Like Casanova, these men too were on-stage; they too marked their little conquests on a score-card. But in the film she had seen, Casanova had at least given pleasure to the women he invariably seduced.

Gopal was the sort, Devi thought, who should make love in a room lined with mirrors. He could then lose himself in the perfect pitch of rapture that delicately flooded his face.

In a house quiet at last, the last of the visitors piled like crumpled cushions on the floor, Devi lay wide awake, her eyes smarting, her stomach still protesting against the whisky and the rich, ghee-soaked biryani. Gopal's snoring whistled like a train across the room.

She thought of the three of them, Mayamma, Sita and herself. Three of the women who walked a tightrope and struggled for some balance; for some means of survival they could fashion for themselves.

Mayamma had been thrown into the waters of her womanhood well before she had learnt to swim. She had learnt about lust, the potential of unhidden bestial cruelty, firsthand. She had had no choices really. She had coveted birth, endured life, nursed death. And she had won some small victory—if you could call it by such a grand name—through that ragged belief she carried within her. She snarls and sulks, thought Devi with wonder, but she has no bitterness. She could live again through Parvatiamma, even through Devi. They were not strangers to her, strange as their choices may have been.

Sita, born fifteen years after Mayamma, was different. She had always been different. Her talent had set her apart from the other girls; so had her unfeminine determination, and the dark brown skin that prospective mothers-in-law had looked at with disapproval.

She had married late, at the ripe age of twenty, when her cousins were already mothers. She had brought with her as dowry twenty thousand rupees, her veena, and a grim resolve to be the perfect wife and daughter-in-law.

She had paid the price for it, not a light one for someone who measured her self-worth so completely in terms of her music. There must have been other dreams, Devi thought, ambitions which had nothing to do with any of us.

In her ruthless attempts to keep these at bay, Sita had built a wall of reticence around herself. This was not a wall that excluded the mundane, trivial or ugly. It distanced her from the ambiguous, and anchored her firmly to the worldly indices she had adopted in place of the veena.

Devi thought of her mother's years of unstinting devotion to the family. How lonely she must have been, and how brusque and suspicious she had been of Devi's hesitant overtures! Her survival, a generation away from Mayamma's, had been far more efficient, but its pain, for all its subtlety, had been just as deep, and perhaps less relenting, because she now looked back on an emptiness unfamiliar to Mayamma.

And I, thought Devi, and faltered in her thoughts. My grandmother fed me fantasies, my father a secretive love. My mother sought me out with hope, and when disappointed, pushed me forward in the direction she chose. You could say I have been lucky, I have been well looked after. I have mimed the lessons they taught me, an obedient puppet whose strings they pulled and jerked with their love.

I have made very few choices, but once or twice, when a hand wavered, when a string was cut loose, I have stumbled on-stage alone, greedy for a story of my own.

But I was too well-prepared, and not prepared at all. America, Jacaranda Road, Mahesh, Gopal. I have run away from all my trials, my tail between my legs, just as I turned a blind eye to my father's helpless thrashing about for an ally, or my mother's lonely hand stretched out towards me.

Devi remembered what Gopal had told her once as they sat on the terrace watching the peacocks dance. He was explaining to her how a mere singer grew into a musician, an artist who knew his mission.

'My guru,' said Gopal, 'was not only a great musician, he was also a very wise old man. He travelled a lot, but whenever he began to feel stifled, when he needed to feel that he could begin all over again, this time on a higher note, he went back to his village.

'He was not very sophisticated and he spoke about his music in the simple, earthy language of the village he grew up in. But his teacher's instincts were finely tuned. He knew exactly when one of his disciples was ready to strike out on his own.'

'And you,' asked Devi. 'How did he know that you were no longer an apprentice?'

'He told me about the silversmith in his village,' said Gopal. 'The silversmith would first fashion several intricate pieces of silver, each separate, with an identity of its own. Then came the more difficult part: he had to weld the pieces together so that each piece became part of one necklace. How did the silversmith know when the fire was hot enough to join the pieces together and make the necklace? He blew into it patiently, with trained precision, through a long, thin pipe, till the fire was iridescent; till it had a life of its own.

'When a pupil of mine,' said Gopal to Devi, 'begins to sing in such a way that he compels me to close my eyes and travel with him, that is the first step. Then, when his voice lights up the darkness with a colour like the peacock's neck, I know he is ready.'

Devi knew the time was right; if she did not act now, she would be forever condemned to drift between worlds, a floating island detached from the solidity of the mainland.

Gopal groaned in his sleep, and turning over, flung an arm across her breasts. She lay still, waiting for him to stir, and when he did not budge, she pushed his arm away.

She got out of bed and looked at him in the dim light that seeped in through the window. He lay sprawled across the bed, no longer snoring, in a deep sleep as still as death.

She picked up the sari she had flung aside carelessly earlier that night. Even in the dim light, the silk shone, shot with a blue-green glimmer. She draped the cloth around her shoulders as if she were trying on a robe for size. She stood in front of the ornate, teak-bordered, full-length mirror that she and Gopal shared, a family heirloom that he had inherited.

She looked into the mirror, but it was as if she was still looking at Gopal's sleeping face. It threw back at her myriad reflections of herself.

Devi undraped the sari and folded it carefully, lovingly, till it was one long, multi-layered curtain. She covered the mirror with the silk so that the room suddenly became darker, and everything, the beds, the table, the sleeping body of Gopal, were themselves again, no longer reflections.

Devi left the silk sari behind, the sari which was the colour of the peacock's neck, when she boarded the train to Madras alone. She had felt bold and carefree when she left Mahesh's house, a little like a heroine. But she felt like a fugitive now, though she was, for the first time, no longer on the run.

The train sped past the countryside, and the landscape outside was dry, brown and unchanging. She looked shifty, she thought, as she eyed the other passengers in the compartment. But after an initial look of mild curiosity, no one spoke to her, or even stared, and she sat huddled on the upper berth, undisturbed.

The city she saw, as the auto-rickshaw rattled its way towards the beach, was festive. It was Diwali time again, just as it had been when she had returned from America. But she no longer shrank back from the fireworks, or the urchins who lit small bombs on the street and jumped away, laughing, when the auto-driver swore and yelled and swerved wildly.

Then, as they left behind the noise and excitement, the bustle of a city in preparation for commercial festivity, Devi saw the long stretches of sand, the road that led towards the house by the sea.

She straightened her back as she saw the house come into view. She rehearsed in her mind the words, the unflinching look she had to meet Sita with to offer her her love. To stay and fight, to make sense of it all, she would have to start from the very beginning.

Suitcase in hand, Devi opened the gate and looked wonderingly at the garden, wild and over-grown, but lush in spite of its sand-choked roots. Then she quickened her footsteps as she heard the faint sounds of a veena, hesitant and childlike, inviting her into the house.

GLOSSARY

agraharam (*agrahara*):	the Brahmin quarter of a village
ashtapadi:	a musical composition, usually on the theme of divine or human love
kolam:	rangoli; a traditional south Indian household does not have a *kolam* at its doorstep only when the house is in mourning.
kriti (*kirtanam*):	a composition, usually on a devotional theme, which forms an important part of Carnatic music
Muthuswamy Dikshitar:	a seventeenth century composer of Carnatic music; his compositions are in Sanskrit, and are generally full of complex allusions.
nadaswaram:	a wind instrument, essential to south Indian temples and marriages
nagalingapushpa:	a thick, large pinkish flower with a

lingam-like pistil.

pati (*paati*):   grandmother (Tamil)

payasam: *kheer*; sweet made of thickened milk

Purandara Dasa: a sixteenth century composer of Carnatic music, whose compositions in colloquial Kannada are still part of classical and folk music.

sampurna raga: a raga that is 'whole', that is, it uses all the seven notes of the scale in its *aarohana* and *avarohana*; shankarabharanam is a *sampurna* raga.

shadja, panchama: the two constant notes (sa and pa) of the musical scale; the other notes are *rishabha, gandhara, madhyama* and *dhaivata* sung as *sa-ri-ga-ma-pa-dha-ni-sa*.

sumangali: a woman who is not a widow; a sumangali prarthana is a puja performed by women for the benefit of, and as thanksgiving for, their status as non-widows.

thali: a chain, usually made of gold, fastened around the bride's neck by the groom in the most important part of the Hindu marriage ceremony. The woman is expected to wear it always, as a symbol of her marital status.

Thyagaraja:

an eighteenth century composer of Carnatic music, the most prolific of all; his compositions, in Telugu, are addressed to Rama.

todi, bhairavi, sahana, kalyani:

ragas in Carnatic music; some of these have broad equivalents in Hindustani music.

The Women's Press is Britain's leading women's publishing house. Established in 1978, we publish high-quality fiction and non-fiction from outstanding women writers worldwide. Our varied and diverse list includes novels, biography and autobiography, health, women's studies, handbooks, literary criticism, psychology and self-help, the arts, our popular Livewire Books series for young women and the bestselling annual Women Artists Diary featuring beautiful colour and black-and-white illustrations from the best in contemporary women's art.

If you would like more information about our books, please send an A5 sae for our latest catalogue and complete list to:

The Sales Department
The Women's Press Ltd
34 Great Sutton Street
London EC1V 0DX
Tel: 0171 251 3007
Fax: 0171 608 1938

Also of interest:

Rama Mehta
Inside the Haveli

The award-winning story of Geeta, an educated, outgoing woman
from Bombay who marries into a deeply traditional family and
enters a life of purdah within her husband's haveli.

A prominent sociologist and the first woman to be appointed to
India's diplomatic service, Rama Mehta (1932–78) was one of her
country's most prolific and respected novelists. *Inside the Haveli* is
her bestselling novel and was based on her own early experiences
as a young married woman.

**'Mehta's sensitive attention to detail pulls the reader in
until you realise with a shock that you are undergoing
the very process of adaptation which underlines Geeta's
journey . . . Mehta brings immense understanding to a
way of life that is rapidly vanishing.'**
Meera Syal, *Financial Times*

**'*Inside the Haveli* is deservedly recognised as a classic . . .
A subtle, sensitive and intelligent novel.'**
Independent on Sunday

'Beautifully written.' *Company*

'Brilliant.' *Cosmopolitan*

Fiction £7.99
ISBN 0 7043 4394 0

Urvashi Butalia and Ritu Menon, editors
In Other Words
New Writing by Indian Women

Fourteen of India's most innovative and acclaimed women writers
make up this irresistible collection. From the harsh realism of
cultural displacement through a poignant vignette of growing up
urban in the eighties, *In Other Words* is testament to the dazzling
breadth and diversity of Indian women's writing today.

**'Surprise is a strong element running through this
collection. The selectors clearly have a nose for a good
story as well as a sensitive ear for the varied voices of
contemporary Indian women . . . A treat.'**
New Internationalist

Fiction £6.99
ISBN 0 7043 4385 1

Kathleen Tyau
A Little Too Much is Enough

Surrounded by countless aunties, uncles and cousins, Mahealani
Suzanne Wong grows up amongst the rich traditions of her
Hawaiian-Chinese family where a little too much is never enough.
But encouraged by her mother, Mahi knows that one day
she must leave to forge her own life. As this time approaches,
she digs deep into the memories of childhood, finding in
remembrance the strength and knowledge needed to carry her
heritage always in her heart . . .

In the tradition of Maxine Hong Kingston and Amy Tan, Kathleen
Tyau weaves the resonant, vivid and often hilarious story of one
young woman's struggle to discover herself amongst her large,
loving and complicated family.

'**Candy-coloured and fragrant . . . Tyau is a beautiful
writer, strong and funny and with a wonderful delicacy of
touch.**' *Village Voice*

'**A feast of a novel. When you are finished, you will push
yourself back from the table, rub your belly and wish
there was more.**' Sherman Alexie

'**Heaven in small bites.**' *The Washington Post*

Fiction £6.99
ISBN 0 7043 4459 9

Sheri Reynolds
Bitterroot Landing

Jael is a survivor. A scrawny wild-child, she will survive her
Mammie's illicit liquor shack and the drunken men who visit. As a
ward of the courts, she will survive River Bill, her surrogate
father who makes her his secret surrogate wife. And she will
survive the fleeting kindness of the strangers who rescue her.

But once rescued, Jael is unprepared for the wider world she
must enter. Only the voices of women, both real and imagined,
make her stronger every day. Until, one day, she is so strong she
can survive without them . . .

For all those who loved the vitality of A Thousand Acres and the
spirit of The Color Purple comes Sheri Reynolds's magical,
inspirational and compelling new novel of redemption, salvation
and hope.

**'Wonderfully compelling, powerful, moving and
complex.'** Booklist

'An original, lyrically written tale . . . Beautifully realised.'
Publishers Weekly

Fiction £6.99
ISBN 0 7043 4462 9

Beth Yahp
The Crocodile Fury

Winner of the Premier's Literary Award

In her youth, Grandmother was a famous ghost-hunter. But she is old now and has lost the power of her extra eye. Instead, she relies on her granddaughter to write down her magic, curses, remedies, wisdom and stories. But granddaughter must also discover the secrets of the nuns at the convent where she has been sent to study and to spy . . .

Spanning three generations of women and covering fifty years of history, from the heyday of colonialism to the struggle for independence, *The Crocodile Fury* is a magical, sweeping celebration of women, culture and power - and has been internationally acclaimed as Malaysia's long-awaited successor to *One Hundred Years of Solitude* and *House of the Spirits*.

'Reading *The Crocodile Fury* is like snuggling into the chest of a loving parent at bedtime . . . It engages all the senses. It is rich with colours and rustles, the shrieks of schoolgirls, soft caresses and sharp pinches . . . It is a marvellous read: sad, funny, clever, witty, lyric and joyous. Our literature cannot but be enriched by the addition of writers like Beth Yahp.' *Canberra Times*

'Amy Tan is to Beth Yahp what a lightly seasoned Chinese soup is to a spicy Malaysian curry . . . Fiery, feisty and as complex as her heritage.' *Australian Bookseller*

Fiction £6.99
ISBN 0 7043 4466 1